Blue Ring Assassins

by
Stephen Cohen

Fictional work based on actual WWII events.

The moral right of Stephen Cohen to be identified as the author of this work has been asserted in accordance with the Copyright, Design and Patents Act 1988

Badman Publishing

The Blue Ring Assassins 1939-1943
ISBN **9798896860563**

Authentic information

Brothel Background

During the second world war, the Nazis decided to re-open a brothel and use the prostitutes as spies, ordered to seduce secrets out of foreigners and catch out disloyal Germans.

The brothel started in 1939, known as Salon Kitty, owned by Katharine Zammit aka Kitty Schimdt.

Walter Schellenberg, a Nazi intelligence officer working for the Sicherheit'sdienst (SD), and Reinhard Heydrich gave Kitty an ultimatum: you and your girls work for us, or you're going to the concentration camps. So, Kitty was ordered to take on 20 extra girls produced by the Nazis, place listening devices in all areas and allocate a listening room in her establishment.

Once all this was agreed, Schellenberg and other SS officers started arresting prostitutes from all over Berlin. They sorted them into the most beautiful ones to train and recruit for the brothel.

The file sent out by Schellenberg to Nazi administration officers stated that they were looking for beautiful, intelligent, multilingual young females who were man crazy.

They were trained by the Nazis to recognise high ranking military uniforms, high-ranking Nazi party officials and foreign diplomats, whom they would then relax with, ply them with alcohol, sleep with them, and extract as much information out of them as possible.

During a British air attack, the salon was destroyed. Schmidt was allowed to re-open in another location, but the Nazi operation was abandoned due to a lack of credible intelligence.

The Blue Ring Octopus (Hapalochlaena Lunulata)

These marine animals are found in the tide pools and coral reefs in the Pacific and Indian oceans, from Japan to Australia.

Small in size and relatively docile unless provoked, they are highly dangerous to humans due to their powerful venom (Neurotoxin Tetrodotoxin).

Each animal has enough venom to kill 26 adult humans, with NO antivenom available.

The venom causes heart and respiratory failure, total paralysis and blindness, and can kill in minutes. Death generally results from paralysis of the diaphragm.

During envenomation the subject is still fully aware of their surroundings but unable to move or talk, thus unable to raise the alarm for help.

SOE (Special Operations Executive)

Prime Minister Winston Churchill's secret army or "Baker Street Irregulars," as they became known. The SOE had several training grounds around the British Isles, as well as in other countries.

Camp X, joint British/Canadian training ground during WWII. Camp **X** was the unofficial name of the secret Special Training School No. 103, a Second World War British paramilitary installation for training covert agents in the methods required for success in clandestine operations

SOE Headquarters were at 64 Baker Street in London.

All agents, regardless of gender, were trained in every aspect of espionage. The SOE had over 400 female agents working behind enemy lines. The use of female agents was considered a necessary factor as they could move around far more easily than men.

Trainees at the camps learned sabotage techniques, subversion, intelligence gathering, lock-picking, explosives training, radio communications, encode/decode, recruiting techniques for partisans, the art of silent killing and unarmed combat. Communication training, including Morse code, was also provided.

Extensive training in resisting interrogation and how to evade capture underscored the gravity of their missions. The SOE operations and research section had to develop some unique devices for their agents. They invented hidden weapons in everyday items such as pens, handbags, umbrellas and navigation devices in such things like lipstick to mention just a few.

Their main purpose was to cause as much chaos behind enemy lines as possible as well as coordinate, inspire, control, and assist nationals of oppressed countries.

Drugs

The use of **methamphetamine**, also known as crystal meth, was particularly prevalent: a pill form of the drug, **Pervitin**, was distributed by the millions to Wehrmacht troops. The effect of the drug would make a person capable of staying awake longer, almost able to ignore injury within realistic parameters as well as make them feel stronger.

Prologue

Hannah

Our quiet countryside home with the bird chorus echoing all around was suddenly shattered by large vehicles arriving, the loud slamming of doors, and shouting from outside.

"Bring them out, bring them all out here now!" someone yelled.

A uniformed soldier entered our kitchen. "Come with me," he growled as he grabbed my arm and led me outside. His grip was so tight that it felt like he would tear my arm off. Screaming and kicking him as we negotiated the hallway.

My Mutter followed, blaring at him to let me go. "Leave her alone, let her go" she kept repeating, but he didn't listen.

As soon as we cleared the doorway, I saw my Vater was already outside, standing in a row, like soldiers on parade, facing the officer who was dressed in the recognisable uniform of the SS. He started questioning my parents regarding their family history. As my Vater replied the officer would tick something off in his book

Unable to see clearly, due to the flood of tears that were filling my eyes and cascading down my face, but I could feel my Mutter's grip on my hand, which was getting tighter and tighter and I could almost sense the fear flowing through her, as if she knew what was about to happen. Looking up at my Mutter, my heart pounding, I had so many questions, but now is not time, as the SS officer was speaking, and we all knew not to interrupt him.

Born to a German officer, I was seen as state property, and as such they were here to take me into one of those girl schools for young Nazis. My parents surely knew this day would come, why hadn't they forewarned me? Twelve years old and taken from my parents kicking and screaming, who could do nothing—for if they did, they would be shot!

"M...m...m... Mutter, help me!" I quavered, "Vater, stop them!" I screamed as I was dragged to one of the vehicles.

"Be strong, Hannah," my parents shouted as the men put me in the truck with some other girls, who, like me, were crying hysterically. None of us knew where we are bound for, But I could see the fear in the eyes of those looking back at me.

Two guards with guns jump in the back of the truck and the tailgate was slammed shut. The large engine burst in to life and with a sudden jolt, we was on our way. This resulted in all of us crying out even louder. It wasn't long before one of the two guard's sitting at the tailgate, stood up, cocked his weapon and shouted, "Quiet, everyone quiet." Initially, his actions only made us scream louder, until he pointed his weapon at us and says "I mean it." The shrieking cries immediately turned to a dull murmur as each girl attempted to stifle their emotions by covering their mouths with their hands or putting their faces down into their arms.

Forty minutes later we arrived at Berlin train station, silently we are ushered onto a train, male and female guards are everywhere, our carriage was already partially full with other girls of our age. This is when we found out what our destination would be. A Nazi school for girls in the south of the country.

I spent the journey reminiscing of my past years at home. As a child, I grew up with my family, just outside Berlin in the countryside. We had what we called a quiet life; we only saw anyone from the Nazi party when we visited the city. My parents voted for them, my Vater worked for them in Berlin, and we all strongly believed that they would finally build a better, more prosperous Germany.

Living in the countryside is healthier; the air is clean, and it is much quieter than the city. Almost every few days we would go for walks as a family through the nearby woods, spotting and naming trees, plants and animals. Immersing myself in the different smells and sounds to me was exhilarating. There is always something new happening in the woods and we would sit for hours watching the animals go about their daily routines.

The school days are short, once home I would do my household chores, some cleaning and fetching of firewood. Once completed, I would go and meet my friend Sabine, who lived close by on an orchard farm. We would play tag and hide-and-seek around the trees, eat apples and I would draw the scenery around our area.

In the evenings, sitting on my Vater's knee whilst my Mutter was knitting, we listened to the Nazi party radio station. The party had some strong idealisms about how they were going to make Germany great again and over the first few years of their leadership they had brought us back to one solid united country, that certainly made us feel proud to be German again.

Often falling asleep in my Vater's arms, I would always wake up as both my parents put me in my bed. My Mutter would run her hand over my face as she tucked me in, kissing me on the cheek and saying goodnight. My world was full of love, joy and playful times.

The train journey was a long one, periodically stopping for more passengers, it looked like the whole train was filled with young people of a similar age to me, both boys and girls. Another two hours go by and yet another stop, this time it was our turn to disembark, in a straight line, we was ordered to follow the female officer to an awaiting bus. A short and silent ride later we arrived at a large mansion, it was breath taking to look at, one of the largest standalone buildings I have ever seen outside of Berlin.

Once off the bus we are separated in to blocks of eight, then one group at a time we are led off in to the building and shown our rooms for the foreseeable future. We are told to change in to the uniform provided and report to the dining room.

I entered with several other girl's; the room seated around two-hundred girls. Told to find a seat we quickly and quietly sat down. The food was simple, but at least hot, some kind of stew.

As soon as we had finished eating, a heavy-set women stood up and yelled, "Attention, attention everyone."

We then had to endure an hour or so of instructions, as well as being informed of the consequences if we did not. Basically, do as your told and you would be ok, misbehave and you wouldn't sit down for a month.

Spending the next six years with a heavy aching heart, missing my family more and more as each day passed, and with more questions than I care to mention. One thing all us girls in this school now had in common was that we had lost our youthful years. Although some of us felt anger towards the state for taking us from our families, there was no room for it to be shown.

The feeling of anger never lasted more than a few moments as it gave way to the much more deeper feeling that we are going to be part of making Germany's future strong, so strong that we would never again be dictated to by other countries; instead, we would be feared!

These schools are some of the strictest and most gruelling places to be educated. The days are long and exhausting, with two to three hours of physical fitness training every day and no contact allowed with the outside world. That is, until you're eighteen, when you are thrust into the world of the Reich and expected to procure a position within the Nazi regime to help build the thousand-year Reich. It is drilled into you that your only purpose in life is to obey the state and your husband, be a good wife and Mutter if that was your calling in the future.

This was Hitler's foundation for the future and one that I personally agreed with.

It was 1939 that I turned eighteen, and that day brought joy to my heart. Given my orders to report to Nuremberg to start my training as a female guard for one of the now many, female prison camps. These camps housed many different people. Mainly anyone who disagreed with the Nazi party regime in any way was imprisoned, male or female. It did not matter about your status in society either.   You followed the beliefs and teachings of the party or you were beaten, imprisoned or killed! Germany had changed so much whilst I was schooled, it had become a much harsher place for non-conformists, and far less tolerant.

I, like many other girls, was taken to the local train station. The school provided all our required papers and some money for food and travel to last for two days. Each person was given the same amount regardless of where their destination was, so we had only two days to report to our new positions.

Standing at the train station in a lengthy line waiting for my turn to buy my ticket to Nuremberg, I couldn't stop my mind drifting towards my family. The urge to visit them was so deep that it completely took over me, so much so that the girl behind me gave me a push as I had not moved up the line.

"Hey, wakey-wakey," she said, as she pushed me softly in the back.

"Sorry, I was in a world of my own," I replied, and as I moved up the line to fill the gap that I had created, we started chatting.

"Where are you going to?" she asked me.

"Nuremberg, and you?"

"Berlin." She replied.

"Oh, my family live close to Berlin, I wish I had been assigned there. And where is your family?" I asked her.

"Right down the bottom of the country," she replied. "I miss them so much! I wish I could visit them but as you know, if we deviate, there will be consequences." Sadness oozed from her face.

"Yes, it's heart-wrenching isn't, but you're right, we have to follow orders," I replied, but couldn't shake the emotions brought on by thinking of my parents who I longed to see again, even for just a few moments.

We were both fighting back the tears now, so much so that I had to leave the line and go to the bathroom to splash some water on my face. My heart was pounding; it felt like it was going to push through my chest. I missed my Mutter and Vater so much.

Returning to the line, I noticed a map showing the train lines and stations around the country. Stopping to study it for a moment I realised that I actually had enough time to visit my parents, if only for an hour, and still make it to Nuremberg on time. I could not pass up this opportunity to see them. In fact, the desire was so strong that I had already made up my mind before I even realised it.

While standing in line, I repeatedly said to myself, "Surely, I am not the only one to do this. There has to be others that have time to visit family and do so!" At the window and without hesitation, "Single to Berlin please," I asked.

My heart was pounding for the whole journey. Was it due to the excitement of seeing my parents for the first time in years or because I was breaking the rules? I really wasn't sure but there was no turning back now as in an hour I would be in Berlin. It wasn't like me to break the rules; I believe strongly in the regime and their future outlook for us, but my desire to see my parents was stronger.

Berlin had not really changed during my time away, apart from all the red flags bearing the Nazi Swastika adorning almost every building and so many shops with the star of David and the word "Juden" plastered all over them, windows smashed in or boarded up and no sign of any occupants.

As I continued to take in my surroundings, the feelings brought on by all I saw and being part of our great nations rebirth made me feel proud to be a German.

Memories surfaced of visiting a couple of these shops with my parents on one of our visits to Berlin. The butchers and the cake shop were gone but I recalled the sweet smell of freshly-baked cakes that lightly stoked your nostrils as you drew closer to the shop, enticing you to follow the smell and sample the delights inside.

The bus ride to my village only took forty minutes. During the journey, I was recalling all the questions I wanted to ask, but most of all I couldn't wait to feel my Mutter's arms wrapped around me, holding me tightly and reassuringly telling me it would be alright, as well as seeing the pride in their eyes when they saw me in my uniform for the first time.

Before I realised it, the bus had come to a halt at my stop. As I walked up the lane, I was remembering all the flowers that would be in bloom, the different colours and strong scent of the roses surrounding our home that I had helped my Mutter plant years ago, the sound of my vater chopping wood in the woodshed and the sweet smell of my Mutter baking bread.

My memories seemed to get stronger and stronger with every step I took towards our home. I could almost feel my parents embrace as I drew ever closer. Now, I could see the end of the tall hedgerow which aligned the gravel road leading up to our house. The feeling of joy engulfed my whole body with every step.

That was until I turned the corner.

Shock and horror took hold of my entire body to the point where I was unable to move for a few moments, my stomach was churning like I had a crazed cat inside struggling to get out. I felt sick and my heart was pumping so fast it felt like it was going to explode. The house was gone! All that was left was a pile of burned-out wood and ruins.

My heart racing, I could feel every pint of blood crashing through my body. I lost all control of my breathing as well as the ability to stand. It was as if all my normal body functions had been snatched out of me.

After several minutes in this state, I realised I needed to regain control of myself and, in a staggering gait, I approached what was left of our home. Everything was gone: family photos, letters from my grandparents, the throw my Mutter and I spent almost a year making for my Vater one Christmas, the blanket my Mutter made for my cradle when I was born. All my childhood belongings and memories, things I had made during my early years with my Mutter and friends, all lost in a blackened, charred mass. That time, now passed, only my memories will keep it alive. The building is covered with ivy and other indigenous plants, so the fire must have happened several years ago.

There was no sign of what had happened to my parents, or even how or why this had happened. Lacking clues here, I decided to walk across the field to Sabine's house, one of my childhood closest friends, to see if they knew anything. Passing through their apple orchard and approaching their house, I could see Sabine's Mutter on the front porch in her rocking chair.

As I drew closer, she recognised me as the young girl she once knew, now as the woman standing before her. "Hello, Hannah," she said, with a big, beaming smile, stepping down to greet me.

We embraced for a moment and I could feel the emotions pouring out of her, the moist feeling of tears running down her cheek onto mine. She had aged more than the years that had passed.

"They have... they have all gone, taken like cattle to the slaughterhouse," she said as she sat slowly back in her chair, wiping the tears from her eyes.

"Yes, I-I have seen our house, everything is lost!"

"Oh, my dear, I am sorry, Hannah, I wasn't talking about your parents. I was talking about my family; the Nazis took Sabine and killed my husband, Wolfgang."

I felt her sadness but, to be honest, I was only really interested in finding out about my parents at this time.

"They took me years ago too. What of my parents, do you know where they are?" My tone must have seemed unsympathetic, laced with only my deepest desire. She stood again, her head slowly moving from side to side with a sorrowful look on her face and tears again running down her face, looking across the yard into the distance.

"They are here, buried beside Wolfgang." She took my hand and led me off the porch.

My parents are dead! I couldn't believe it! Anger rose like a volcano from the deepest parts of my soul. Why? They were peaceful loyal people. The tears running down my face are only interrupted by the tightening of my stomach, my legs once again turned to jelly, and thoughts of never seeing them again raced through my mind.

We headed through the orchard towards the end of their property, where I knew there was a small building in which Sabine and I played in as children.

"People think that Hitler and his Nazi party are going to make Germany great again, but they know nothing yet of the price we will all have to pay, Hannah." A great sadness in her voice but I disagreed and spoke up.

"They have done so much already. They have taken back parts of our country that were taken from us during the war. They have restored our pride and made Germany great once more, a country to be revered!" I had been taught this at school and believed it.

"Oh, Hannah, I hope your eyes will soon be opened to the reality of our world."

"My eyes are open; no one but the Führer could have accomplished such great feats."

We continued our walk in silence, drawing closer to a building. As we passed it, she gripped my hand tighter, and we came to a patch of lush green land. Standing at the edge for a moment, she lifted her arm up slowly and pointed to the corner of the grass and there I saw three small crosses.

"Here they are, they are with Wolfgang. He buried them, Hannah. We found them inside the house. They had been burned so badly and we didn't want to leave them there. I am so sorry. Then, when Wolfgang was killed by the Nazis trying to stop them taking our Sabine, I thought it would be better for him not to be alone."

"How did it happen?" I asked as I knelt by the graves, clutching the ground, with the most overwhelming feeling of a deep void in my heart.

"I believe it happened the day you were taken, Hannah. We don't know why. We saw the smoke and raced over to your house but there was nothing we could do; the house was in flames."

Daisies grew nearby, and I picked a few and placed them on my parents' graves. We weren't a religious family so saying a prayer over them would not be necessary - I simply said, "I love you" and as I passed Wolfgang's grave, I thanked him for what he had done.

We walked back to the house in complete silence, arm in arm. I couldn't believe my parents had gone or why this had happened to them. We embraced for a final time and wiping the tears from our eyes said our goodbyes. There was nothing for me here now. I walked down to the bus stop in a soulful, devastated daze. Speaking only to the bus driver to get my ticket, I returned to the Berlin train station.

With grief and untamed thoughts troubling me, I had lost all concept of time. Sitting in one of the cafés close by the station, I didn't even realise that the day had turned into night, completely unaware of my surroundings, just sitting staring into my coffee, which by now was cold, thinking of my parents and why they had died.

As part of the school-training we had been taught to control our emotions, to be devoid of feelings, to carry out instructions without question! But I was struggling with this concept right now; they don't teach you how to deal with the loss of your entire family. The instant overwhelming cascade of emotions that were now constantly running through me was unbearable, I was struggling to regain control of my thoughts and emotions.

Suddenly I was thrust forward from behind, catapulting me back into reality, sending my coffee and the table flying. Those close by had already started moving due to the ruckus going on, not wanting to become part of it and instead heading for the door. I landed on the now upturned table, putting my hands out to save me from hitting my face on the table legs.

I quickly got to my feet and as I turned around, I saw four or five men dressed in the black uniform of the SS. They were the most brutal of the Nazi party. Yes, all Nazis could be violent, but these men had a particular passion for it. They had special training and would not waste a moment in hesitation before killing you.

They were fighting to get a hold of a young lady, about the same age as me, who was, in fact, putting up a good fight against them. I really don't know why or even if I thought about it, nor of the possible consequences, but once on my feet I went to the soldier's aid.

"Stop fighting!" I shouted at the young woman, "they will not hurt you if you stop fighting."

Before I knew it, I had been arrested myself and we were both placed in a truck. Why, I didn't know - I kept asking, but my questions fell on deaf ears. All they kept saying was that it was state business.

The thing that was going through my mind right now was why this woman was still alive? Anyone I have ever heard of attacking an SS officer was normally shot on the spot - something wasn't right!

"Are you stupid or something?" The young woman asked me. But before I could answer one of the guards got up and kicked her in the stomach.

"Keep quiet. No talking," he barked as he returned to his seat.

Seeing how quickly punishment was metered out, I decided to stay silent. Besides, I was now lost in a deep feeling of déjà vu. My last journey like this was back when I was taken by the SS from my parents. Although the Nazi schooling had taught me to honour and respect Hitler and the Nazi Socialist way of life, those embedded doctrines were becoming more distant as the hours passed and the images of my parent's house and graves constantly flashed in my mind. What I was seeing here and the echo of Sabine's mother's words in my head were unsettling.

After about an hour, we arrived at what seemed to be some sort of training or military base close to Brand-Briesen. It was small though, only a few buildings, but the security was vast, wire fences and lookout towers all around. There must be a landing strip close by as I saw a small plane coming into land.

It felt like one of the camps we had seen pictures of at school, like a prison camp!

We were ushered into a room of the larger building, into what looked like a surgical room. Panic hit me like a train, engulfing every essence of my body, already emotionally stretched to near breaking. A woman in an SS uniform came into the room. Mid-forties, I guessed, overweight but muscular, she had a stern look about her, purposeful and determined.

"Right, strip!" she ordered.

Well, that wasn't new to me as we had to strip all the time at the school for medicals, but this had a sense of danger that created an unease.

She walked around the two of us, looking up and down at our bodies with cold, uncaring eyes for our discomfort, repeatedly saying, "Very nice, very suitable," before carrying out a medical examination on me then the other woman. Eventually, we were told to dress and the questions started.

"Do you like men?" Strange question, I thought but I replied "yes", as did the other woman.

"How many men have you had sexual encounters with?"

My companion replied first, "I am a prostitute, I have lost count."

I could feel this look of bewilderment coming over my face at where this might be going.

"I am a virgin; I have just left a school for girls run by the regime," I replied then continued, "I was on my way to Nuremburg to start my training as a prison guard, here are my papers."

The woman snatched them from me, glanced over them, then she simply tore them up, daring me to say anything. I realised I was totally in their powerless.

"Yes ma'am, whatever the state requires," I said dutifully.

With me compliant, she turned to the other young woman.

"What is your name?"

"Regina Braun, ma'am."

"Age?"

"What, you can't guess my age, I always thought you people had special powers," Regina, replied with a smile on her face.

"Less of your back chat, you will do exactly what you are told to do, or you will be shot! Now, what is your age?"

She didn't reply, she just simply glared into space. I could see the anger building in the officer's face.

"What is your age?" she asked, looking at me.

"18," I replied.

"How many languages do you speak?"

"Four."

Without saying a word, she glared at Regina who, knowing that the same question was coming, answered.

"Three, treis, tres," she replied in English, French and Spanish.

"You are German right?"

"Yes," Regina replied.

"Then you speak four languages."

"And?" Regina simply replied.

This response just had the woman shaking her head and mumbling something as she left the room. "GET DRESSED" she shouted as she slammed the door behind her.

In her absence, I felt able to speak. "What is wrong with you, Regina? You need to stay calm or you will get yourself into trouble."

The young woman turned to me, showing spirit, "Oh really? They don't scare me, I have been fighting against these Nazis for over five years now, I hate them."

This was dangerous talk and could get one killed. I needed to distance myself. "Do what you want, Regina, just don't drag me into anything. I don't want to die. Just do as they ask; it will be a lot easier for you."

"I am not like you, a yes person, following every instruction without question. Are you a dog, do you want me to stroke you behind the ears?" she taunted.

"You're trouble! I believe in the Reich and will do my duty as requested."

We were interrupted when a guard opened the door.

"Come with me," he said, directing us to follow him down a corridor into a large room where there were about another eighteen girls, all about the same age, looks and body structure. What are the SS going to do with us, I thought as the guard told us to sit.

Moments later, a very mean-looking man entered the room. You could tell he was a proud man; he was well groomed, and his uniform was spotless. Not bad looking either! about twenty-eight years old.

"My name is Walter Schellenberg, and I am second in command of the SS Reich Main Security Office. You have all been selected for a special mission in the name of our beloved Fuhrer." He let that sink in for a moment before continuing. "While you are here, we will provide for all your needs. You will be trained in all aspects of espionage." Glances were exchanged among us women. "You will not talk to anyone about why you are here or what training you are doing. You will not interact with the personnel in any way. And you will obey your instructors and my staff at all times." He went on to add, "Anyone who does not comply will suffer the consequences, which will be long and painful. Consider this a warning!"

Schellenberg was well known; he had no children, but his marriage to Kathe Kortekamp, a seamstress three years older than him, was in all the papers. It was last reported he had to divorce her due to her meaningless job, her social standing and her age.

Since 1933 he had performed many successful intelligence missions in France and Italy. He spoke several languages and had moved up the Nazi ranks very quickly, making a name for himself as an extremely brutal man, which looking at him and the calm way he spoke you wouldn't have thought that for a moment.   At the school we were kept very well informed about the high-ranking officers of the Nazi party; it was part of our weekly curriculum.

With the inspection and lecture over, we were all shown to quarters. Four beds in each room, on which the same-coloured nightgowns – all white – and a nondescript ill-fitting uniform that didn't reveal to which faction or government body we belonged to.

It was a sleepless night for me as I spent most of it thinking about my parents. I knew that I wasn't going to be allowed to grieve, so I decided to hold tightly onto the fact that they would be proud of me for doing my duty as was expected by every loyal person in the regime.

Morning arrived with the sound of very loud banging on the doors to rouse us, as one of the soldiers made his way down the corridor. I looked at my watch - it was 05.30.

Six weeks in, and I could now strip, clean and rebuild a small firearm (Mauser HSC); it's small and easy to conceal. My target practice was coming along nicely too; I could now group my shots quite closely. In fact, I think I am now a much better shot than my vater, I could see him smiling in my mind. The intelligence gathering aspect, learning how to use certain questions to manipulate the answers was remarkably interesting. I found I was enjoying elements of the training and was willing to learn.

The day came when everyone gathered in the large room, waiting patiently until one of the instructors came in and bade us to follow him. A different part of the complex where we had never been - a long corridor with rooms, not one of them with a door; inside, a single bed with a mattress. Singly, we were directed to enter a room and strip completely. Staff entered and took our clothing away. This was puzzling and a bit unsettling. Of course, I knew this was part of adulthood, but I couldn't help thinking how this would or even could benefit the Reich. Orders are orders, and as a member of the party I must obey but this one confused me.

My breathing was now completely erratic, my hair was clinging to my face from the sweat. My emotions and imagination were running wild, made worse by the sound of soldiers marching into the large room next door. I could feel every inch of my body trembling, I heard the large room door open but that was all, no voices. Almost instantly, I was confronted with a naked man standing in the doorway.

I sat on the bed to hide my body and didn't know where to look; the sudden realisation that I was about to be taken made me feel sick inside. What was I supposed to do? This was the first time I had seen a naked man, let alone have one touch me, or me touch them. The embarrassment of not knowing what to do and the fear in my eyes must have been visible to him through my blushes and uncontrollable shaking.

He slowly walked towards me, gesturing with his hands to calm down. We could not talk at all during this process, but my body language gave every emotion I was feeling away. He sat next to me on the bed. I knew I had to do this! He started to stroke my skin gently. Each stroke felt tender, caring, as though he was trying to put me at ease.

Of course, I knew how this worked, but I had never actually done it. After a brief period of time, he started kissing me and I seemed to instinctively lay back. I still had no idea if I was doing anything right. He laid on top of me, his hands were now all over my body. I just laid there and let him do what he was doing. I had a strange feeling of passion come over me for a while—that was until he pushed himself inside me. It felt strangely natural, but somewhat uncomfortable at the same time.

I was glad when it was over. We just laid there, waiting, until we were told to go. The instructors were constantly walking up and down the corridor, watching us all throughout the whole time. It felt degrading, unnatural even.

I guessed that Regina had no issues with this part of the training, but she was always getting herself into trouble and arguing with the staff. Two weeks ago, she was lashed by one of the instructors for attempting to leave the compound. She was constantly swearing at everyone, very loud and noncompliant.

Everyone was still wondering what we were training for. We had spent a lot of nights and some days talking about nothing else. I had developed a small gathering of friends which helped to pass the time away. Each of us struggled with some aspects of the training, so we helped each other in the areas that we are weak in.

One girl, Heidi, was brilliant at all the technical training, but I could see she struggled with the physical training so we would practice on our down times with the help of Petra, who seemed to master this part of the training very quickly. To escape the training we would sit peacefully, Heidi produced some nice poetry whilst I would do portraits of some of the girls, standing in front of the Brandenburg Gate in full Nazi party uniform.

The morning following my first sexual encounter, I woke early and was fetching coffee and rolls from the kitchen to tide me over until official breakfast, when one of the instructors told me that today was our last day. At last, we would find out what all this was about.

After group breakfast, which consisted of coffee, cold meats and some fruit, we all gathered in the large room .and waited patiently for the arrival of Schellenberg. He marched in with a rather well-dressed, middle-aged lady, who regally took a seat at the front. She created quite an impression, wearing a large flowery hat and decked out in jewels. After a congratulatory speech at completing our training successfully, he introduced the grand, mysterious lady.

"This is Kitty Schimdt, whom you will be working for."

She stood and simply bowed her head and said, "You may call me Madam Katharine."

Now, the girls in the room who had been prostitutes, knew immediately what this was leading to; the rest of us had an inkling. We were going to work in a brothel, the sex part of the training making sense finally. I felt a little more at ease about it now as the other girls told me it's always painful the first time but gets better, so lie back and enjoy it.

"As of tomorrow, you will be working at Madam Katharine's salon. You will do exactly what you are told to do and with whoever we tell you to do it with." Schellenberg continued. "The salon is wired with hidden microphones and we have men in the cellar listening. If you attempt to leave, you and four other girls will be shot, so you are all reliant on each other."

The message sunk in. We would be expected to inform on anyone talking of leaving, a matter of self-preservation.

The rest of the day was spent going through piles of clothes that had been brought in for us. We were to pick out two to three outfits each, and they also gave us a small bag of make-up to start us off. I didn't really like the outfits. To be honest, I don't think many of us did, but they were all we had to use for the time being.

When Heidi and I noticed that, yet again, Regina was absent, we went to find her before she got into trouble. Too late, for as we left our building, we saw her being dragged out of one of the smaller buildings along with one of the soldiers. They were only partially dressed and must have been caught in the middle of some sort of sexual encounter. As it wouldn't have been officially sanctioned and likely that Regina sought some benefit from it, there would be punishment. I couldn't believe it; we were finished and about to get out of here and she went and did that. The soldier was taken away to the compound office while Regina, half-naked, was held for the arrival of Schellenberg. He ordered the guards to take her back inside the building.

Heidi and I didn't escape notice, nor did the others who had come outside as well. We were ordered to follow a soldier who took us to the same building. We were pushed into a room. It was a small room and not a lot of places to sit. When the soldier locked the door, we all started to worry.

"What is going on? Why are we locked in?" someone behind me asked, I think it was Heidi but couldn't be sure as we were so tightly packed together.

Regina

As he secured me, his face was so close to mine that I could feel his breath, with a hint of garlic from his last meal, on my face. The smell mingled with a cologne he used – sweet and sour together. The ropes around my wrists were now cutting into my skin, and even the slightest movement caused me excruciating pain which was difficult to stop, as my arms were suspended by a chain from a hook in the ceiling. Job done; the guard left the room. The only thought running through my mind was what was going to happen to me.

I was shaking with fear, yes. Being hit and whipped was not a novelty; to be honest, I was sort of used to pain, but I couldn't shake the feeling that this was going to be somehow far worse. Had I gone too far this time?

The room was not like the others in the building we had spent the past few weeks in. It was dark, cold and smelt of something I had never smelt before, not unlike that of cut meat sitting on a counter in a butcher's shop. Thinking it was a little used building was why I had chosen it for the assignation with the soldier, but I hadn't been in this far.

"We have warned you time and time again about causing disruption and trying to escape," spoken from a darkened corner of the room, which startled me, I thought I was alone.

I couldn't see who it was, but I recognized his voice. It was Walter Schellenberg, second in command to Reinhard Heydrich, the chief of the SS Reich Main Security Office. The main function of this office was to rid the Nazi party of any kind of opposition, regardless of how small it was or who it was. There was no sphere that was not under the ever-watching eyes of their organization and they had complete autonomy to use whatever methods they wished to deal with any kind of hostiles, be that an individual or an organisation. One thing most people knew about these two high ranking officers was their lust for brutality.

A match flared in the darkness as Schellenberg lit a cigarette. He paced up and down with measured unhurried strides, unbuttoned his jacket and removed it. There was enough light, and my eyes were becoming accustomed to the gloom, for me to see him carefully fold it and place it on a chair. He turned to face me, locking his eyes on mine as he rolled up his shirt sleeves. It was then that I realized I was about to endure more pain. He moved closer, to stand in front of me. I could not look into those cold, heartless black orbs that were his eyes. He had devil's eyes! Like a dog, I am sure he could sense fear!

Without a word, *thwack!* Schellenberg's backhand struck my face, leaving me with a bleeding nose, the taste of copper on my lips as it dripped over my mouth. He hit me again, so hard that I was finding it hard to hold my head up straight. Again, and again the blows, my blood now covering his hands. He grabbed my hair and thrust my head back. My vision was now obscured by the swelling on my right eye. He looked at me and just nodded his head with a satisfied look on his face. I briefly had the thought it was all over and he was satisfied with a lesson of a beating. Until he walked behind me and ripped my clothes off, throwing most of them to the ground just below me, in an effort to catch and soak up the pool of blood now forming. I did not want to think about what was coming next. He walked back to face me, wiping my blood from his hands with some of my clothes, looking at me as he did so with an emotionless, lifeless face.

"I see the scars on your back have healed nicely from your last encounter with the guards; you should have learned from that."

"Go and......" I stopped myself completing the sentence, but for just a moment my fear had turned to anger.

"What was that? Did you say something?" turning his head so his left ear faced me.

He moved to a table in the middle of the room and picked up a small-handled piece of round dark wood. I couldn't really see that well, so I thought it was to beat me with. Coming in close, he hit me in the jaw with it and I heard a crack before excruciating pain hit me - it was like having toothache in every tooth, the agony seemed to creep slowly through my entire head.

"Now you won't be able to answer back or cause trouble for a while." He had broken my jaw.

He walked behind me; I was expecting to feel the sharp pain as he hit me with the wood again. Instead, it was the lash, several times. I couldn't keep count, the pain from my jaw was now overcome by the pain coming from my back, it felt like he had opened my flesh to the bone. I lost consciousness.

The blessed peace of being out of it did not last. As I was coming around, I thought I had been dreaming, as the first sensation I felt was that of a man inside me. *Had I fallen asleep on a client?* I thought. Then the pain hit me, I opened my left eye and he was now going at me like some wild bull. Every violating thrust feeling like some sort of tool ripping at my internal skin. Every time I attempted to vocalise my pain; I was hit with the agonising pain from my jaw. He was taking me apart, one piece at a time!

I kept trying to go somewhere happy in my mind in an effort to mask the overwhelming feeling of fear that now gripped my consciousness. It was probably a good thing that I couldn't speak as I know I would be calling him all the horrific names that I could muster, even though I know it would result in him hurting me even more, just the thought brought a little inner smile to me, he hadn't yet fully broken the rebel in me.

"Looking at the state of your face, you are finished as a prostitute, but your body looks okay and still works fine. Well, the front of you anyway."

Schellenberg lit another cigarette and smoked it halfway down. He moved towards me and, using it as a tool of torture, started burning my skin around my nipples. His motions were slow and meaningful. Each burn left a blister as he followed the circle shape of each nipple.

"Now your body is starting to look like your face," Schellenberg hissed.

I couldn't really feel any part on my body now, it all felt the same, unimaginable pain coming from every inch of my body.

I don't know how many hours went by as I passed in and out of consciousness as Schellenberg used me as his plaything. I was exhausted and in so much pain, I could not even plead for my life and now I just wanted death. My whole body hurt; I just wanted the pain to stop. Schellenberg secured his belt and pulled his gun. I lost consciousness again. Schellenberg was not about to shoot me whilst I was unconscious, that just would not provide him with any satisfaction or feed his lust for inflicting pain and suffering.

The last time I regained consciousness, not knowing what to expect, I only knew I wish I had not. My mind and body was broken, the pain unbearable.

"So, you are awake. You have caused nothing but trouble ever since you arrived here, and now I am going to make an example of you."

He placed his pistol close to my left eye.

"Dirty whore," he said.

I had the feeling I had beaten him - the dark tunnel of the barrel was a welcome sight as I eagerly awaited the bullet that would end my suffering. He wouldn't know he was delivering me from pain and fear. He hadn't broken my spirit; well, I wasn't about to let him see he had.

I didn't hear the shot and suddenly I didn't feel anything anymore....

Hannah

We knew instinctively what the muffled sounds coming through the door meant. I understood why Schellenberg had chosen to do it all in a room close by. It was all a psychological game. A hard reality crept into our future, wedged in by the muffled tortured cries coming from Regina. We had had to listen for hours, intermittent noises, moans and screams and periods of silence.

I wasn't sure if the noise echoing in my ears was real or part of some daydream as it was fighting for its existence against all the screaming around me, I opened my eyes and looked around and saw the truth in the expressions on the faces of those enlarged eyes staring back at me. Fear, total fear engulfed us all.

I now realized our fate was sealed, the fear was obvious and conclusive.

My thoughts were suddenly interrupted by a loud bang, a single gunshot! I was now overcome with shock, am I dreaming? Is this now the world I live in, one of torture, rape and murder? My world is turning inside out, my once love for the Third Reich is becoming overturned with total fear for any uniformed officer! The very regime that I swore an oath to, is beginning to show me it's truth.

"He fucking killed Regina!"

"Bastard!" someone screamed out.

"He fucking killed Regina," Petra said again, "One of us is going to be next," she said in a horrified, scared voice..."Why else would they lock us in here?"

"Be quiet! Do you want them to come in here?" I shouted, the fear in my voice was surely heard and felt by everyone in the room because they immediately shut up.

Everyone now expected the worst. For several hours they left us in this small room with no water or food. The stagnant air that filled the room carried with it a sweet but sweaty odour which was suddenly overcome by the smell of urine. Not surprisingly some of the girls had soiled themselves. No one said a word, we each understood it might well happen to us next. In times like this I found myself always going back to my parents, remembering what they always taught me, *if you do as you're told, you will not get into trouble*! This was also a constant during my school years.

The silence was more terrifying than the noise of him beating Regina. We were all subdued now. The shouts of murderer merely an expression of emotion stoked by fear and anger, but mostly fear. The click of a key in the door as it was unlocked was like the cocking of the hammer of a gun and several girls whimpered. The door was flung open and the now fetid interior air rushed out which made the guard cover his nose.

"Everyone out," the guard shouted. We hurried outside, fleeing the claustrophobia and welcoming fresh air and daylight. We came to an abrupt halt, fixated by Schellenberg, calmly standing by a truck smoking a cigarette.

He didn't have to speak, merely held his hand out, showing us his palm. When we were still and mesmerised by this blood-streaked figure he spoke in an ominous tone. "Now, so that everyone fully understands what will happen to them if you don't comply with instructions." He moved slowly to the back of the truck. "This is what will happen to you." Throwing open the back of the truck so we could all see Regina's naked body, covered in blood and lifeless. I felt someone grab my arm tightly from behind me, I glanced back, it was Heidi.

"You leave in an hour, go and get ready," he ordered.

We all instinctively took off running like we had been released by a starting pistol, not a word was spoken whilst we all hurried to gather our belongings, eager to flee this hellish scene and the memories of the past few hours.

Chapter One

The Brothel

We travelled in two trucks back to Berlin and arrived at Giesebrechstrasse what looked like a large hotel in the middle of a block of buildings. Madam Katharine came out and we followed her inside.

The hotel was quite large with many rooms, well furnished, with moody lighting and silks everywhere. There is a young lady dressed in a maid's uniform in the reception area. On the left a parlour room with heavy set sofa's and two more ladies dressed in cocktail dresses. As we climbed the stairs, I saw some girls scantily dressed, with German soldiers on their arms heading up another set of stairs, the pungent smell of stale tobacco and alcohol hit my nose.

We were shown to our rooms. We had to share with someone, which did not matter to me at all. I was sharing with Petra, one of the girls I had given a portrait to at the training camp. She had also helped Heidi and me with the hand-to-hand combat training, so I already knew her, which made it easier.

Our room had two beds, a wardrobe, and a small dressing table. We both sat for a few moments on our beds, just taking in our surroundings and situation.

We had to be careful what we said. Remembering what we had been told, listening devices were placed in every room and soldiers were in the basement recording every word. I could not help but wonder what it must be like for those soldiers in the basement, listening to people having sex all day. It must have affected them in a sexual way to start with but after a while becomes quite tedious!

We started to unpack, which didn't take too long as we didn't really have many personal items and as we did, we started chatting about our assignment.

"So, this is our life now Hannah, unfairly paid Nazi bitches," said Petra.

"I like that black outfit, Petra. We are about the same size, what do you think to swapping outfits from time to time?"

"Sure, I don't mind that, having only three outfits could be a little boring, so let's agree there's an open house on clothing then."

"Works for me, Petra. Do you think we will get any time to ourselves? You know to go sit in a café, have a coffee and some pastry maybe?"

"How would I know, Hannah - like you this is my first time working in a brothel."

"Sorry, I thought you had already been working as a prostitute!"

"Yes, I come from the streets, but I have never worked for anyone before, I took care of myself."

I felt a little sorry for Petra, not that she portrayed she needed or wanted any sympathy, but it must have been an extremely hard life, living on the streets with no one to call family.

Madam Katharine's regular girls must also be wondering what is going on, with another twenty new girls now all fighting for the same clients.

Suddenly our door swung open and one of Madam Katharine's girls came in. She started looking at our things, picking up make-up from the dresser and going through our clothing.

Without any kind of introduction, not even a hello, we could feel the resentment filling the room.

"You have some wonderful things, can I have this?" she asked, holding up some lipstick as she looked at Petra.

Without thinking she reacted. "No, now get out and don't come back," she replied, snatching the lipstick out of her hand and pushing her out the door and slamming it shut.

"Shithead," the girl shouted through the closed door.

Petra stood, glued to the spot, clenched fists with her face turning red, like she was about to explode. "That pisses me off; I hate bullies and beggars," angrily replacing her lipstick on the dresser.

"Well, I can see you can take care of yourself Petra, and that's some street mouth you have."

"What are you? My Mutter? You learn quickly on the streets. What you have, you keep and don't let any fucker take it from you."

I could see the passion in her eyes as she said that to me.

"I saw that you can take care of yourself whilst training. You seemed to enjoy the fight training."

"Sometimes you have to fight back, Hannah."

"Maybe so, but we all must follow instructions, Petra."

"You're one of those, a yes bitch, follow without question, your Fuhrer will deliver, whatever!" Petra replies in a defiant tone.

"We are all property of the state, Petra. My parents always taught me to follow instructions, from them as well as from the regime, we must obey."

"Really? You follow your path. I will keep doing what I have always done."

"And what is that, Petra?"

"M-m-my life has not been like yours, Hannah, and I don't like to talk about this fucking stuff." There was a short but definite pause. "My parents - died, in a car accident when I was five! I ended up with a couple down the street from our home, that was until I was fourteen years old, now I fight for or take what I want from life. Are you fucking happy now?"

"I am sorry to hear about the loss of your parents, Petra," I said with a lump in my throat and fighting back the tears, as I was instantly reminded of my own grief and the feeling of been cheated out of spending my life with them! I continued, "I know how much that hurts; I lost my parents when I was twelve."

"My parents' death was overlooked by the regime; I am pure Aryan but the couple I had lived with were in fact Jews. I had been out and as I was returning home; I saw my guardians beaten and put in the back of a truck. They were bound for a ghetto or prison camp or worse. I ended up working the streets to survive until like the rest of you I was arrested and forced into this new chapter of our lives."

"You lived with Jews?" I said in a shocked voice

"They are nice people, caring, and they took me in when no one else would." Petra stated with an aggressive tone of voice.

"Petra! They are not even people; they are gutter rats!"

"It's best you don't say another fucking word about them, Hannah, you might not wake up in morning! We are not all brought up to believe the Nazi policies are true and correct," she replied with an extraordinarily strong meaningful tone.

"I think your parents' death has misled you, sent you down a wrong path, Petra."

I thought it best not to continue this line of conversation as it was clear to me that we had different views on this matter, besides, it's really easy to kill someone while they are sleeping and I certainly had the feeling that I wouldn't be her first.

My thoughts were suddenly interrupted by Petra taking out the portrait I had done for her and hanging it on the wall. She clearly has some emotional issues; yes, she can have strong opinions on some subjects, but there seems to be a softer side in there, we have also both gone through pretty rough times.

Life at the brothel was hard. We spent months having to tolerate many men throughout the day and fighting with the other girls to keep what we had. They did not seem to like that we had all the high-ranking officers and high society clients and attended all the big parties, whilst they had to put up with the normal run-of-the-mill soldiers. Resentment in the ranks was setting in.

"We have another party tonight, Hannah; do you know if it is here or at someone's home?"

"I really don't know, Petra. One thing I do know, it will be full of the same boring people that we have to get drunk, and have them paw all over us."

I went off to check on Heidi; she didn't seem to be managing so well with brothel life and her roommate could be horrific with her tongue, so much so that even Petra started sticking up for Heidi. Heidi was the quiet one, reserved even, more of a thinker than anyone in this place. She just got on with things, didn't really say much or interact with many of the other girls, and also seemed to take far too much notice of the technology being used in this place by the regime.

We have to keep our doors open when we are not working, it's a constant flow of traffic going by, some girls with clients, some are just walking around awaiting their shifts. As usual, two of Madam Katharine's regular girls came and stood in our doorway, I readied myself for yet another confrontation.

"Look here, two high class meat grinders," one said to the other.

Meat grinders was just one of the terms they used to describe us. Others included 'low rent male jockeys' and 'Hitler's whores'. Petra was quick to respond as always with some colourful loud language. As for me, yes, I was learning the art of saying what I mean but with a tempered tone.

"There is a hell of a smell all of a sudden, Petra."

"Yes, some shitty bitch needs to get a bath, Hannah, and quickly."

"What is it with these girls, Petra? I know girls can be bitchy, I certainly saw, and was guilty of it myself during my school years. Back then I always thought it would ease off once into adulthood, but to be honest, its worse!"

"Hannah, it's just life and in this situation mainly fuelled by jealousy."

Madam Katharine was constantly having to get between us and the other girls to prevent any actual fighting, although sometimes she just wasn't around so some girls ended up with black eyes. One even got a broken nose.

Those that fought got smacked about by Katharine to keep them in order, but a few slaps were not deterrent enough to stop some of the stronger-willed girls. I for one was not about to let anyone hit me; besides, I was quite good at blocking a potential hit and throwing my aggressor to the ground. I actually found it a release, after days of being mauled by different men which disgusted me to be honest, I enjoyed unleashing some of my frustrations.

"Are you ready to go down to the waiting area, Petra?"

"Yes, Hannah, let's begin yet another day."

Our days are mostly the same - wake around eleven am, have a little breakfast, some bread and cheese, that's if there is some cheese. I then get washed and dressed which I can usually take my time with as clients don't normally start arriving until late afternoon. One of the best parts of the job is when clients bring food in with them, it's a nice treat as its mostly home cooked, bread, cookies, cake and sometimes even caviar.

By mid-evening the brothel is generally full of very drunk men. Come midnight we close the doors for the evening, and as clients slowly drift out, we clean up our rooms and ourselves, then it's downstairs to clean up and re-stock the bar ready for the next day. It can be early morning when we get to bed, which is why we sleep in till late.

As we walked down the stairs, I noticed some of the girls just stood around, huddled like school girls in corners, giggling, I could only guess what about, their last client, the size or performance of him or, as in many cases, they could just be talking about us.

"Do you know what happens to anyone that is found not been faithful to the Fuhrer, Petra?" I said, to be overheard.

"They are taken to one of the camps aren't they, Hannah? They get totally fucked up!" she replied, playing along.

"Actually, some are shot or hanged for treason and anti-patriotism."

"How do you know that, Hannah?" she asked. "And like I said, they can get totally fucked up!"

"I overheard a couple of officers from the basement talking about it in the bar. One of them mentioned a name of an old client of mine, he was shot because of what I had reported."

"Serves them right," Petra whispered in my ear as we walked down the stairs.

Although I agreed with the principle of what we are doing, after all any regime is only as strong as its members, I do think that killing people just for having an opinion is a little extreme, but then I guessed we will all pay for questioning, in one form or another, our beloved leader.

We walked down the stairs and into one of two reception rooms. When Madam Katharine was not around, she appointed one of her long-standing girls to run the front of house. She was under strict instructions to select the higher-ranking officers and high society clients to our reception room.

This, however, did not always go to plan due to their hatred of us and from time to time they would send us normal everyday soldiers. Of course, we could not refuse, otherwise we could give ourselves away, our true purpose that is!

Today was one of those days and the girl she had selected was one of the worst, she would send in a normal soldier for every five clients or so throughout the day and almost every one of them would be violent or want something out of the ordinary.

About four hours had gone by. I was with a client in our room and suddenly I heard what I thought was a pistol shot, followed a few seconds later by screaming. I hurried to put some clothes on, my client had already rushed out of the door and was nowhere to be seen.

As I entered the hallway everyone was trying to look inside one of the girl's rooms. I pushed my way to the front and looked inside, there was a man holding his left side with blood pouring through his fingers and in his left hand his pistol. I could see there was a female laying on the floor motionless but could not tell who it was.

I hurried to find Petra and Heidi, hoping that it was not one of them. Petra, as it happens, was making her way up the stairs. And Heidi was down in the reception area.

"What happened, Hannah?" she asked me.

"A client has been stabbed and he shot the girl, she is dead, I think," I replied.

"Anyone we know?"

"I couldn't see her face, Petra. As long as it isn't one of us though!"

It wasn't long before the whole place was swamped with local police and SS officers. We all watched as they brought out the girl on a stretcher. That quite easily could be one of us one day, I thought to myself. The man was helped down the stairs and taken to a doctor.

From the conversation we could hear as they helped him down the stairs, he had asked the girl for a certain service, she refused, he hit her, she stabbed him, and so he shot her in the head!

"Serves him right, it was only a matter of time before one of us retaliated, these men treat us like meat, continually hitting us, bruising our legs and arms as they brutalise us," Petra whispered to me.

It was a stark reminder to all of us - this is what can happen, if you refuse a client. We are whores and they are mostly members of the Reich and we cannot refuse them anything. This was brothel life. As the months passed, I saw several incidents like this. It was as if the soldiers were using us as a release for their anger and frustrations.

Chapter Two

Berlin 1939

Schellenberg arrived at the brothel for one of his many inspections. All microphones would be turned off when he arrived. He always ensured he reinforced his hold over us on these visits. Although he didn't care who he picked on, there was always someone left with a permanent reminder of who he was.

Any clients in the residence would hurriedly dress and leave unless they were of higher rank, but even they knew not to cross him or try to interfere with him.

On this particular visit it was my turn; he entered our room and Petra went to leave.

"Stay where you are," he barked, slapping his horse whip against his leg.

He moved around our room using his whip to pick up items of clothing or push things around on the dressing table.

I am sure he could feel the shaking of our bodies through the floor; his mere presence instilled fear in us and he knew it.

"Strip." This was one of his methods of selection. If you hesitated even for a second to comply with him, then you would be on the receiving end of his wrath.

Both of us immediately undressed. I had slightly more to take off than Petra and so took slightly more time, which made me the object of his frustration. It was all a game to him.

"You are both incredibly beautiful women. Genuinely nice indeed, you look clean and well fed."

"Thank you, sir!" we both replied as his eyes slowly scanned over the naked curvatures of our bodies.

Our nakedness could not hide our inner emotions as every part of our bodies gave away our fear with uncontrollable shaking. My shaking was by far, worse than that of Petra's. His eyes moved over my body as he scrutinized each slender not frail inch. My figure although suggested a disciplined strength, continued to shake uncontrollably.

"Turn around." He prodded me in the shoulder with his whip.

I closed my eyes, readying myself. My heart was now beating so fast and fear gripped me so deeply I could feel my stomach churning to the point where some sick came up in my mouth. Without hesitation I returned it from whence it came and just in time.

Thwack across my back, the sting of his whip hitting my naked skin instantly stopping my shaking which gave way to the pain. Again, and again he whipped me. I fell to my knees, tears running down my cheeks. My screams could be heard throughout the brothel.

Schellenberg never said a word, and the next thing I knew Petra was covering me with a sheet and shouting at someone to get the medical kit.

Heidi soon arrived with it, as though she had been ready and waiting, and again it was nice to see Petra's softer side.

"That cruel bastard will get his dues one-day, Hannah, mark my words," Petra said, in a truly meaningful hatred tone.

"Why must he do this, Hannah? He already knows we are all scared to death of him," Heidi remarks in a soft Muttering-type tone.

I found myself asking related questions. There just seemed no reason to beat people that you already have full control over; it just seems excessive to me. He always made sure not to damage our faces or the fronts of our bodies as they were not only our assets, but his also. He had accomplished what he set out to do, keep and reinforce our fear of him.

On 1st September 1939, Germany had invaded Poland and the hatred for the Jews and other minority groups was now in full swing, antisemitic ideology and policies gripped the country. The past few years had seen them lose all rights as people. They had had everything taken from them, and in some cases even their lives. Prison camps and concentration camps are popping up all over the place and bursting at the seams. It was a different world we now lived in, filled with death and destruction. We were at war! This action had not only affected those being persecuted but also everyday citizens. Rationing of certain items was introduced; clothing, shoes, certain foods, and soaps were now in short supply. Although working for the SS did have some benefits, they ensured we had a good supply of soap and alcohol because if we were not clean, we couldn't work, and if we couldn't work, if we couldn't loosen the client's lips with alcohol, then they would be less willing to let something slip, and then no intelligence would be gathered.

Life at the brothel was slower now, as most members of the armed forces were busy with invading and plundering other countries, and many of the girls spent their time sitting around chatting, doing their hair, but we still had a steady flow of clients, mostly high-ranking officers and their companions. The soldiers in the basement were becoming less friendly towards us; they resented their post and believed they should be at the front, so much so that they started drinking heavily and as a result kept forgetting to record us.

To be honest this did not matter as most of the intelligence we had gathered was meaningless to the Nazis, it all seemed a waste of time to me and to others too.

Madam Katharine had become less approachable and careless. She spent most of her time in her room and so some of the girls took advantage of the situation and started using bully tactics to get clients. They now knew to leave us alone; they had come to understand that we had been placed there by the SS, as well as being trained to fight with deadly precision.

After several months, things seemed to settle down again and by the summer of 1940, we started to see an increase in the flow of clients again. Something had changed though; in the men I mean. They seemed far more dogmatic, and cold, that was, until they had half a bottle of brandy.

One other change we noticed was their total belief in ultimate victory. I, for one, fully understood, what we, as a country, had to do to regain our status around the world as a great nation, but not all the girls agreed with the regime's approach, Petra for one. Even

I was beginning to wonder if it was worth the price, we are now paying in the form of all the dead, the suffering, the destruction that has now been left in our wake.

Another change that was very scary to us all was that for the first time we actually heard and saw the effects of war. The British RAF had started dropping bombs in and around Berlin. It was 25th August 1940 a night I will never forget, but one we would all become used to. Some of us started to organize bombing drills in small groups, so on our down time we would practice getting down to the basement as quickly as we could, collecting each other as we went. It was something that became part of our everyday lives, but there were some girls that just thought we were been silly. They thought that even though it was already happening that Berlin would never really be affected by the war. How naive!

Berlin's night sky took on a completely different look since the bombing started. In total darkness it was as if we were transported into another world. On cloudless nights, Berliners had the privilege of actually seeing thousands of stars, something they probably never witnessed before due to the lights of the city obscuring their view.

Of course, that all changed as soon as the search lights went on and they started scanning the night sky for their quarry. Not long after the lights the night would fill with the *boom, boom, boom* and *rat-a-tat - tat* sounds of the guns. In a different time and place the trails of light that the bullets caused as they raced towards their targets would have looked quite pretty.

Over the following weeks and months this became more and more intolerable. The months passed by and as they did the bombing of Berlin increased and became more sporadic. The Allies started out targeting the industrial area, but by the end of the first year they just started carpet bombing the entire city.

We all knew it was just a matter of time before it was our turn. Hitler had turned a once great city into a pile of burning buildings and rubble, all because he started bombing London in the hope of defeating the British and their stiff upper lip mindset - even his top generals were against bombing London. We were all paying the price for that decision now and I couldn't stop the thought that maybe this time his generals were right! For the third maybe fourth time in my life, I found myself directly questioning the actions of the Reich. The price was becoming too high, even women and children's lifeless bodies are scattered or merged with fallen buildings and left to rot in the streets. Never before have I seen so much death, the stench was almost overwhelming.

Over the past few months, I have found myself becoming more and more cold of heart. Nothing seems to bother me; the sight of constant death and injury, not just in the streets but in the brothel on a weekly basis has turned my heart and mind dark and unsympathetic.

Only last week, two girls were shot on our landing by a soldier who then shot himself in the head; we just picked them up and put them in the street, cleaned the floor and went back to work. It can take a few days before the bodies are removed by the police; they are busy with other far more pressing issues now. A couple of dead whores are way down on their list of priorities.

Heidi seemed to be bothered by all the death the most, and it seemed to introvert her even more. To help take her mind off the death and destruction, now surrounding us, we would sit and spend some time writing poetry and drawing, with Petra our biggest critic, but we did find out she was a particularly good chess player.

July 1942. The allied aircraft pilots must have loved the sight of Berlin burning, I imagine it looked just like London now. Payback can, in times of war, be a beautiful thing... For them it must have looked beautiful I guess; the sooty smoke that plumed into the idle clouds, the sprawling ruins of concrete and twisted iron works in the streets below, bursts of fire shooting from the crevices in the debris. It was all a sort of art to many of us witnessing this transformation of our cities.

The dutiful RAF pilots headed for home after yet another successful bombing raid on Berlin. The first bombs had screeched past the top of the brothel with a terrifying whistle. When the café beside the brothel shook violently, I could hear the sounds of the airplanes overhead, and I knew it wasn't the summer breeze that carried it. What I did in the next few seconds would mean either life or death for me.

Heidi erupted through our door. Her blonde hair was wet, and it stuck to her face like dried seaweed. She was wearing nothing but her underwear. Her lips trembled and her eyes burned with fright. I had been sitting at our dressing table moments ago applying the dark red lipstick provided by the SS, when the mirror shook, distorting my reflection. It had momentarily turned my face into a shimmering multiplication of images. I had to steady it, stiffened in fear I listened out. There was a crack, like thunder, rumbling and vibrating our building as a bomb hit close by.

"Otto's café is in ruins, we must move!" Heidi shouted at us; it was the first time I had ever heard her raise her voice. But you could hear the urgency in it all the same.

In the small hallway behind Heidi there was a confused mishmash of footsteps and screams as the other girls scuttled about in what can only be described as total confusion and fear for our lives.

"It will be bad this time! I can feel it, Petra."

"We must go! And now, Hannah, move your fucking skinny ass!" She shouted. Her street survival skills had kicked in. Petra's voice was lost in the approaching drone of even more aircraft.

"Get the other girls," I said breathlessly as I forced my legs into a pair of black trousers.

I could hear the droning of the aircraft engines getting louder as they got closer. Petra looked at me; her chest heaved up and down, half naked, she hurried around the room. Her legs trembled. I thought to ask her why she was not properly dressed, but such a question would have amounted to a type of misnomer at this time, and place. We had to get to the cellar!

"Cellar, cellar, cellar!" I cried, as we ran down the stairs, momentarily stopping to look around for some of our group. The shouting got louder as we progressed downwards, more and more girls gathered. "CELLAR, CELLAR!!"

We had made it to the lobby where I noticed Chuska crouched under a desk in complete fear. As I looked into her eyes the walls and windows splintered into what seemed to be a million pieces, and as they fell around us, the whole area filled with dust, I was thrown around like a rag doll.

The whole building was now unstable, I could barely see the wooden door that led to the cellar, my ears had a constant dullness to them, and my eyes filled with moisture as I tried to look through the dust for the others.

"Everyone okay?" I shouted out.

I saw that the walls were riddled with holes. A picture of the Fuhrer that hung on the wall had shattered; the glass was a web of splinters with shards sticking out like stalagmites. All traces of Hitler were gone, except the hailing hand.

"Holy crap..." someone shouted and screamed.

I saw Heidi who had been cowering under her own arms. She was peering with large and veiny eyes across the wreckage at me. Her mouth was contorted in a pitiful ugly curve.

"Holy crap..." she moaned.

"Are you okay?" I asked her.

Her eyes seemed to be fixed in one direction. I followed Heidi's line of sight along the floor to an angle by the desk where Chuska was crouched seconds before. There were broken pieces of glass around the general area of the desk. I then saw a black shoe and a pale leg, blood snaking away from the disarray that surrounded her lifeless body. The noise of the aircraft was coming back. It was far off but the whistle of more bombs falling was unmistakable. I felt every muscle tense. We would surely die if we stayed where we are, we must move and quickly.

"*Hannah, Petra, Heidi...!*" someone called from upstairs.

"Down here! We're down here!" Heidi hollered.

"We have to move," I said urgently.

"What about the rest?" asked Heidi.

"Not our fucking problem Heidi," shouted Petra as she grabbed Heidi's hand.

There were twenty-nine other girls in the brothel. Some were surely still up in their rooms, filled with terror and *foolishness*. They ought to be down here with me and the others; that was why we had practiced so much for just such a time. Their fate lay in their own hands now.

As I looked back at Heidi, I notice her face was covered with blood. The cuts on her head and face must have come from the glass shattering.

I heard the rumbling of running footsteps and screams from upstairs as some of the other girls started making their way down.

Bombs were dropping again outside; this was no time for heroics. The booms drew ever closer and the wailing of the wounded filled the darkness.

Suddenly the cellar door flung open and I saw a single arm gesturing in a hurried fashion, I told Petra to grab Heidi's other arm as we made our way down into the darkness of the cellar.

The explosion above was like nothing I had ever experienced before. The world around us shook as though we were about to be engulfed. Another direct hit above us, I stumbled down the steps into the damp darkness under the brothel, screaming as a bright smouldering blaze sought to engulf me. I fell on top of Heidi among the old furnishings and wine cases, toppling a table with bottles on it. The crash of the bottles was lost in the sounds of the explosions above. I had hoped that I would not be taken by the war, other than what it had made of me by circumstance. There was a brief intermittence, screams filled the cellar, in that high-pitched shriek that was the constant domain of women in distress and fearful.

Had it all been a dream? My life and all the pieces of the puzzle that had led to this moment - would I wake up at home and find my parents in the kitchen making breakfast and preparing for the day ahead?

The cellar was engulfed in flames as above us, yet another bomb went off. I felt something hit my head and I was flung back into something soft, then there was burning, a searing and I was plunged into darkness and silence as I lost consciousness.

Chapter Three

Brand-Briesen Airfield, Just outside Berlin 03:40

Officer Helmut

I was filled with adrenaline and fear as I attempt to navigate through the hail of bullets from both my fellow comrades on the ground and the RAF machine guns housed in their bombers.

Flying at night is a dangerous occupation, but even more so under these conditions. I often wished I could be hit, but just enough to be grounded for a while so I could have some respite from the constant fear of dying.

I wasn't a fighter pilot, but I wished I was to be honest; dying as a fighter pilot, serving my country would be an honour, but instead I am part of the intelligence core, reconnaissance, attached to the Sicherheitsdienst counterintelligence division run by Schellenberg. My job, at this time, was to report on the damage caused by the allied bombers, I truly wished they would give me a chance for some payback! But no, I only observe, and report back the vast destruction of my beautiful city. The airfield was part of the training grounds that we had been trained in, and it was Schellenberg's retreat whilst Berlin was under siege.

The airfield itself was a narrow strip of rugged sand and stones with thorn bushes at its perimeter. The office house was a tin box, a rushed contraption from the look of it, situated at the end of the runway. Behind it was the dark foggy landscape of pine forest, its floor filled with snow in winter and it looked resplendent and beautiful to behold. But this was summertime and yet despite a war ranging around us, it was still quite a beautiful place.

Landing at this airstrip at night was risky, just as much as flying at night. With only a few small fires as guidance you could easily get it wrong, and no matter how many times I did this it scared the hell out me.

I brought my plane to a stop as close to the office as I could. A single sentry stood at the door as most of his comrades had been killed or injured. I noticed as I flew over the camp that it had been hit several times; many of the buildings now billowed with flames and smoke.

The sentry performed his normal salute and I returned salute and entered the office.

Schellenberg's secretary, a pale looking lady, sat in the outer office. She had short black hair and bright eyes, red lips and long eyebrows, and her desk was bare of everything except a stack of files in the middle of it and a telephone with the handle stuck between her shoulder and rosy cheek. She stopped talking when I entered. She looked past me at the door. I took the hint and shut it.

"Officer Helmut to see Officer Schellenberg."

"Welcome, Herr Helmut," she smiled. "Please sit, he will see you in a moment."

The girl continued talking rapidly, in a pure provincial German dialect. She was about 27 or so and not bad looking. I stopped looking at her when she stared back at me. She ended that call and the phone started ringing again at once. She listened briefly, looked over at me and dropped the handset back on to its cradle.

"He will see you now." She waved at a door behind her.

"Danke," I replied, with a hint of a smile.

I opened the door to a small room. It was more a living room than an office, one of the small luxuries the Reich bestowed on top officers such as "the man with the heart of stone". Walter Schellenberg lounged on a sofa, stretching his legs out before him. A glass of clear liquor hung carelessly from his hand. On a table beside him there was bottle of schnapps and a telephone. The walls were finished in a grey colour and a single painting hung on the left, a Vermeer. I had truly little knowledge of art, but the work looked particularly good. On the wall just above Schellenberg was a picture of the Führer.

"Please sit," Schellenberg said quietly after running his eyes over me with an expressionless face. Schellenberg was well known for his brutality, not just to those who resisted the Third Reich but toward everyone who crossed him really. He ruled through fear.

"What is the situation?"

"Severe air raid, and Berlin is in flames, mein herr," I replied.

"That pisses me off," Schellenberg growled, as he poured himself another drink, a vein twitching on his temple and his left eyelid flickered just imperceptibly. He sipped from his glass and gestured at me with the bottle, I picked up a glass and he poured me a glass of schnapps.

"Stupid asshole," Schellenberg blurted out angrily, referring to Hitler I guessed. "We had all warned him this would happen, but he never listens..."

"What of the brothel?"

"It is difficult to ascertain. It looks like the building was levelled, sir."

Schellenberg threw his remaining schnapps down his throat and I did the same. The alcohol burnt its way down and caused me to shiver internally. Schellenberg picked up the telephone and asked his secretary to put him through to Heydrich in Prague. I could only hear one side of the conversation, but it certainly didn't seem a pleasant one. After a few minutes Schellenberg slammed the phone down.

"Son of a bitch!" he said, loudly and angrily. Schellenberg was becoming more and more frustrated as time passed. "Right, we will have to get to Berlin, and fast. Can we use the airfield there?"

"Yes, I think so, mein herr."

"Then you will fly back to Berlin. Take the doctor with you; I will inform the ground commander you are coming and acting on my orders."

"Yes, mein herr, and what are your orders?"

"You must see if there are any survivors, and if you find anyone alive, bring them back here."

Schellenberg picked up the phone again to his secretary. I couldn't help but feel elated; finally, I am given a chance to do something constructive.

"Inform the doctor he is going to Berlin and he is to report here immediately."

A brief time passed, and then a short, greying man stepped into the room. He wore wire rimmed glasses and carried a small hold-all under his arm. His stethoscope hung around his neck. He shook his head and sighed deeply before settling his bag on the floor.

"Berlin, mein herr? Why must I go to Berlin? What of my duties here? We have many men who are injured!"

"You have met all the girls and can identify them - you must bring anyone that is alive back here, understood?"

"Jawohl, mein herr."

Even though dawn was now breaking, the doctor wasn't looking forward to the fifteen-minute flight; he didn't like to fly.

"Inform the ground commander at Staaken Berlin they are coming," Schellenberg instructed his secretary, and stood watching as we both left the building and got into my plane.

Soon we were over the heart-breaking catastrophe that had happened to Berlin earlier. Flying through towers of dark smoke as we fly over the city, I looked down and could see little more than destruction, the streets full of rubble and burning timbers, the sadness that filled my heart was overwhelming! We landed, took a truck with five men and headed off towards the brothel.

The doctor looked at a skeletal structure that used to be a church, most of it was now a pile of bricks and wood, smoke, and fire. Beside it was another building, it used to be a school. It had also been flattened and its pillars were flung in the middle of the road, all around was nothing but sprawling ruins of destruction, concrete, and wood, entangled with lifeless bodies. My sadness soon turned to anger, and now even more, I wanted a fighter plane!

He looked past the soldiers waiting in the distance. Behind them a car smoked; it was on its back and one of its melted tyres still turned. Houses burning on either side of the road. The brothel was back there somewhere. It was hard to recognize the area; everything looked the same now. Dazed survivors scavenged the ruins, anguished cries rang out all around, but no rescue mission was in effect yet, it was everyone for themselves.

Hot brick hissed, a few fires still burned from the ruins and it was not certain where the entrance to the brothel was anymore. The devastation was vast and incisive, the air filled with the smell of burnt flesh, rubber and ash. Every breath was followed by uncontrollable coughing, the air is so thick it was making my eyes stream. The bombers had been thorough.

Chapter Four

The Brothel is in ruins

Petra

I came around first. Dazed and confused, I fumbled around in the darkness trying to ascertain where everyone was.

"Hello, cough......cough...hello, is anyone there?" I tried to shout with a dust filled voice. "Hannah, Heidi, where the fuck are you?" My mumbles went un-noticed.

I then saw a small, dim light coming through the rubble. So, I pushed against it and managed to make the hole big enough to let some more light in. Clearing the dust from my eyes took a few moments but once my eyes got use to the light, I turned around to survey the dust filled surroundings for Hannah and Heidi. I saw what I thought was Hannah's legs, covered with smouldering wood and brick. I wasn't really sure why I was doing this; after my parents' deaths, I vowed never to let anyone in close again. I never wanted to go through the emotional trauma of losing someone close to me ever again, but these two girls had become a major part of my life.

"I am coming Hannah, I am coming, oh please don't be dead." Coughing and spluttering as I scrambled towards what I thought was her.

I carefully removed the still hot charred wood from close to Hannah's back. I noticed a little movement and a muffled but decisive screech. She was severely burned but alive.

"Hannah, Hannah, help! help me! Someone fucking help me!" I shouted out but no one responded. I was alone, I continued to dig her out and as I did, I could see Hannah was badly burnt.

I moved her a little closer to the hole and laid her down on her side that wasn't burnt; she was in a bad way, but certainly breathing. I then heard who I thought was Heidi cry out, "Help, cough...cough I am stuck!"

"Heidi, is that you? I can hear you; I am going for help!"

"Is that you Petra? Get me the hell out of here! Have you found Hannah?"

"Yes, she is severely burnt but alive. I am going for help Heidi, hold on!"

I frantically but carefully pushed at the surrounding wood and brick until the hole was big enough for me to climb out. I got halfway out, and something fell and hit me in the back of the head.

Dazed, I manage to climb out, struggling to stand or see anything, my head bleeding, I hear someone shout.

"There, there...look!" STOP.

"That's one of them!"

"Who? That half naked whore wandering about falling over everything?" one of the guards asked, pointing with his finger at a ragged, cut and bruised female staggering about amongst the rubble.

"Yes, come on, help me!" he replies.

I could hardly stand, whatever had hit me on the head must have knocked me out for a moment. I do not remember falling, as I came round, I did recognize the doctor from the training many months ago.

"My friends, help my fucking friends. They are stuck down in the cellar," I screamed, hoping I was pointing in the right direction. Several soldiers hurried off and started checking the area.

They must have found a hole and two of them jumped in. A few moments later one of them pops his head out and shouts over to us,

"I have found five mangled bodies trapped under a concrete wall that looks like it formed part of the exterior structure, everything is mangled and twisted," Helmut shouted.

Another six charred bodies which are impossible to identify, their blackened backs glued to the floorboards which still smouldered beneath them are found among the smouldering rubble.

"We have found more!" shouted another soldier as they slowly surveyed the rubble.

"Curious," said a hard-faced Gestapo guy who had joined the rescue, as he pushed a large smouldering piece of timber aside to reveal a pile of bodies. There were body parts everywhere, some burnt, some simply crushed under the rubble, it was impossible to tell who was who.

"Why are we searching for a load of fucking whores?" one of the soldiers asked.

Helmut took out his pistol and shot him.

"Anyone else got any questions?" he shouted and continued, "We are acting directly on Schellenberg's orders, anyone who questions that will meet with the same fate. Understood?" placing his pistol back in its holster.

"Quiet, everyone shut up I can hear something," Helmut shouts turning his head and trying to lock on to the sound. Finally, they found the hole that Hannah and Heidi were trapped in.

"Hang on girls, we are coming," Helmut shouted into the hole.

"Help...cough..me, help me." A frail voice replied from the darkened, dusty, burnt-flesh-smelling hole.

Helmut

I climbed down into the hole and came across a brunette-haired young lady with burns to her left side. She was unconscious; I carefully lifted her out to the other soldiers who placed her on a stretcher and took her over to the doctor.

"My name is Helmut," he shouted. "Who else is in here?"

"Over here, please help me. I am stuck under some wood," a gravelly female voice replied.

"I am coming, what is your name?"

"Heidi! Please get me out of here, I don't want to die! I am trapped under a pile of wood, get – get me out of here!"

"Keep talking Heidi, I will follow your voice, are you hurt?"

"I have some cuts and bruises, please hurry, I am scared to death of dying under all this!"

As I reached the distressed women, my eyes now adjusted to the dim light and I could see her blonde hair matted with blood and dust, and two blue eyes peering out from a blackened face.

"Okay, okay, I am here," quickly lifting the timber and rubble off her.

"Get me out of here, please hurry! How many have you found alive?"

"Only you three so far," I replied.

Petra

At the truck the doctor had sedated Hannah and bandaged Heidi's cuts on her face,

"Right. We must get these girls back to Camp Brand-Briesen, as instructed. I will drive the truck, Helmut, you get back to your plane. Thank you for your help," said the doctor.

"Is Hannah going to be alright Petra?" Heidi asked, anxiously.

"The burns look bad, but she is strong - she will make it Heidi."

"How are you doing, Heidi?"

"My face hurts, Petra, do I look a mess?"

"Your face is covered in bandages Heidi; you have looked better," I replied, putting my arm around her to comfort her.

As Hannah slept through the lull we were driven back to the camp. She was lying down on her side on a solid surface, the vehicle rocked from side to side, sometimes violently—at other times just mild bumps and jolts, but every movement resulted in pain for her. Even though she had been sedated, the pain resulted in her opening her eyes widely from time to time. We were on a small country road now which had not been tarmac, it is very bumpy and I was sure that the doctor was hitting every hole on purpose.

The truck made another turn and entered the compound where we had been trained many months ago. Both Heidi and I could hear and smell the fires before we could see them. As the truck came to a stop, I could see that this place had also suffered from the bombing.

"Right girls, help me get her inside," the doctor asked.

Hannah woke up when someone pulled at her feet. She almost bawled from the sharp pains coming from her body. She bit down on her clothing to hold in a guttural scream, shutting her eyes tightly and groaning. The pain must be excruciating.

Heidi

"Sorry, Hannah, sorry but we have to move you," I said in a soft voice, been careful not to pull at the burnt skin as I steadied Hannah on the stretcher. Entering the building I immediately recognized the room, it was the one they had used during their first examination, but now it was filled with injured soldiers.

"Get her on this table." The doctor gestured towards a large metal table like that of an operating table. "Come with me, girls."

We followed the doctor into another large room where there is several beds and a sink.

"Get yourselves cleaned up and I will return as soon as I have dealt with your friend."

"Her name is Hannah," I replied.

During the next couple of hours, we cleaned and tendered to each other's wounds, and looked through the soldiers' lockers for clothing we could use. Petra could see I wasn't in a good place mentally.

"Heidi, do you remember at the training camp when Hannah got an infection?"

"Yes of course I do, Petra. She was quite ill."

"Did she just give up and lay in bed all day?"

"No, Petra, she was up on time every day and completed the days training, just like the rest of us."

"There you are then, she is a fighter! she is strong, she will be ok! So, lets focus and getting ourselves sorted out."

"Of course, you are right."

The doctor entered the room and asked Petra and I to help bring Hannah back to the other room. He then placed a needle into her arm and ran a small pipe from an IV stand. "This will help her."

"Is she going to be ok?" Petra asked.

"She is a strong one, she has a lot of fight in her, she will make it," the doctor replied and then continued, "Now, let's take a look at you two."

Several days passed and although everyone could hear the drone of aircraft in the distance, we felt safe for the time been as this camp had already been hit several times by the bombers.

"What are you going to do now Heidi?" asked Petra.

"I was just reminiscing about an old boyfriend actually!"

"You had a boyfriend before all this?"

"It happened whilst I was at school. I would sneak out during our down time and we would sit in a nearby forest and have a picnic, or go for long walks; those were happier times."

"Where is he now? In the military?"

"Yes, sort of. What about you, Petra, and love?"

"Nope. Everyone that gets close to me dies, Heidi."

"Hannah and I aren't dead!"

"There was a guy that I use to see, I think he only thought of me as something for pleasure, like most men, to be honest. I went to him for comfort, closeness, you know, when you need to feel special. He treated me well, then I was arrested and thrown into this world."

"What are your plans if they let us out of here?"

"Well, I don't know about you, but I am getting the fuck out of here as soon as I know Hannah is okay," whispered Petra.

"Petra, remember what happened to Regina. We must be careful; I do not want to go through that."

"There has to be a way. I have to get away from this situation, Heidi, and I don't give a shit how."

"Look at me Petra. Just talking this way, I am shaking with fear."

Petra moved closer and gave me a hug. "It will be okay Heidi."

We had not seen anyone else apart from the doctor and his other patients in the other room for several days now, not even Schellenberg. He must have been busy with the current events and situation.

That evening Hannah came around; although a little groggy from the medication, she was at least conscious.

Hannah

"Where am I? Petra, Heidi are you there?" Hannah mumbled.

"I am here, Hannah, we are at the training camp, the doctor has taken good care of us," replied Petra.

"What has happened to me, I can't feel a thing?"

"That will be the medication, Hannah." Petra then continued, "You have been burnt quite badly! Your left side only, your thigh just above the knee, left hip, the left side of your torso including part of your left breast, the upper part of your left arm and small parts of your neck and cheek close to your ear. You are going to be okay but it's going to leave some scars." She wiped away a tear and fought to hold back her full emotions.

"Drink some water, I will get you a little food." Said Heidi.

"Food, I don't want food! Look at me, I look like a piece of over cooked meat, and that smell! What is that smell?" Anger and despair now took over every inch of my mind.

"Take these, the doctor said we should give you these pills if you wake up." Heidi handed her two white pills and some water.

"What are they?" I asked.

"They will help with the pain Hannah, please take them." Replied Heidi.

The pills are strong, within thirty minutes or so I was moving around surveying my surroundings, I couldn't feel a thing, it felt like I was flying. I realised where I was; one of the buildings from our weeks of training. I spent most of the night taking painkillers and looking at what used to be my nicely curved body with soft skin - now covered on one side with melted, blacked smelly flesh! I could hold back the emotions, not just the continued crying but in my head, all I wanted to do was die, no one is going to want to look at me now, let alone be close to me. Around 07.00 am the doctor arrived.

"Hannah, good to see you up and about," said the doctor.

"Why didn't you let me die! you should have let me die!" I asked, with tears again running down my face.

"I am a doctor, it's my job to save life, not take it."

I pulled out the bottle of pills I had been given earlier.

"How many of these have you taken?" the doctor asked. "You can't take too many of these Hannah, do you know what they are?" asked the doctor.

"They stop the pain, I need them." I replied.

"These are Pervitin, a methamphetamine. In small doses they will help with the pain yes, but in large doses are extremely dangerous and highly addictive. We give these to our front-line soldiers. They tell me it makes them feel invincible."

"Look at me, I have to live looking like this for the rest of my life, a piece of over-cooked meat! I am trying to come to terms with this fact, as well as the pain!"

"In time the pain will stop, your body will heal, you can still fully function, you are alive and that's what you should be focusing on Hannah. You must only take six a day, no more, and only for the next couple of weeks or so, okay?"

I said nothing and returned back to the room were the other girls had already woken. The doctor went on to treat the soldiers in the other room.

"Morning girls," I said as I entered the room.

"Oh, Hannah you seem in a better mood this morning," replied Petra.

"Well, I have had time to consider my situation overnight. I now realize that my life is going to be different from now on, but I can still be of use to the Reich."

"Are you serious Hannah? Look what they have done to you, I think you need to do some real soul searching," replied Petra, continuing, "Heidi is a nervous wreck and cut to pieces, you're burnt to shit and still talking about jumping back onto a sinking ship?"

"What are you talking about Petra, we must fight for what we believe in. Look at those soldiers in the next room, they have not given up. As soon as they can, they will be back fighting."

"And for what? So, they can give their life for their country? Look around you Hannah, Berlin is in ruins and the British are not going to stop bombing."

"I have always believed Germany could be great again, Petra."

"But at what cost Hannah? Look at you! look at what they have already made us all give, our families, our loved ones all gone as a result of one person's idealism. Get a grip on reality you stupid bitch!"

"I need to think, Petra. Nice to see the situation has not caused you to lose your street mouth; in fact, it seems to have become worse."

I couldn't tell the others just yet, but I have been in conflict for some time now regarding my beliefs in the regime. Over the past months I have fought back any negative thoughts regarding them, I didn't want to let my parents down. But now, maybe it's time, to start thinking about myself for a change.

"Are you leaving us, Petra?" asked Heidi, continuing, "where will you go, what will you do?"

"Well, I want out, yes Heidi, I fucking hate it here, and I fucking hate them with a passion. I have decided that if I am to die as a result of this war then it's going to be on my terms, doing something that means something to me!"

"What do you mean, what are you going do?" asked Heidi.

"Payback, starting right here. I am going to kill as many Nazis as I can, in any way I can, Heidi."

"But how are you going to do that Petra?" asked Heidi with a bewildered tone in her voice.

"Heidi, you are beautiful but sometimes I wonder if you are missing a little something sometimes. Open your fucking eyes girl."

Petra and Heidi continued talking, I needed to get out of there and think. My mind was racing with a thousand questions, my body hurts like hell - well it seemed like a thousand question when in reality it boiled down to one: did I love my country?

As I walked around the now crater-ridden smouldering camp the hours passed by as I contemplated that very question. I came to a strange but enlightening conclusion that yes, I loved my country, but could I stand by and watch it be destroyed - but not by the British? Petra was right, our country had been destroyed from within.

I headed back into the building to find out what Petra had in mind.

"Petra, what is your plan?"

"This is the way I see it, Hannah, we have to start fighting back, take some control of our own destinies, for our country and ourselves, and we start right here and now."

"The changes we dread most

may contain our salvation."

—Barbara Kingsolver, *Small Wonder*

Petra

"Look around, we have everything we need. We all passed the weapons training they put us through, yes? Now due to everyone in the camp being injured by the bombing there are plenty of weapons around: handguns, rifles and knives."

"Yes, I did, but I have never shot at anyone, let alone killed someone," replied Heidi.

"Think of it as target practice Heidi; point and shoot," I replied.

"We can't kill them all, not the doctor. He has been kind to us. We can't kill the doctor," stated Heidi.

"If he is against us then he dies, no one here can be left alive otherwise they will hunt us down. Do we all agree?" Waiting for their response.

Everyone nodded in agreement and armed themselves with whatever weapons they could find in the barracks and surrounding rooms.

"So, here is the plan. We wait for the doctor to complete his treatment of the soldiers. Whilst he goes off for his morning coffee I will go in and start seducing one of the soldiers, you two pretend to be preparing medication and bandages. What I am doing should be enough to get all the others attention. When I give the signal, we shoot them all. Heidi you're on look-out duty, let us know when the doctor leaves."

"Okay, Petra."

"Hannah, you are by far the better shot; can you handle two pistols?"

"I will give it a go, Petra."

"Your head is on straight about this Hannah, yes?"

"Don't worry about me, Petra, I've got this."

"The doctor has left," whispered Heidi .

"Okay girls, give him a few minutes to get back to his room."

We waited for five minutes to ensure the doctor had settled into making his morning coffee. He normally had his gramophone playing, so he wouldn't hear the shots.

"One final weapons check, make sure they are well hidden. Once we go there is no turning back."

"Let's get this over with," said Heidi.

"Morning boys! How are you all feeling? We thought we would come and see how you are all doing, if you need anything?" asked Hannah.

Those soldiers that could, started whistling and clapping and sat up in their bunks, smiling with eager anticipation as they watched me start seducing one of their comrades.

Hannah and Heidi took up positions around the room with hidden sidearms ready to spring into action. The soldiers started cheering; they were now fixated on me.

"Now!"

Almost, but not simultaneously, we all pulled our weapons and fired. It was over within seconds; even Heidi did her part.

"Right, let's get some fuel and douse this place ready for later. As you two do that I will go and see the doctor."

"You're not going to kill him are you, Petra?"

"Heidi, stay focused on what you have to do."

The war raged on in the distance. I could hear the drumming hum of flying aircraft and the intermittent thumps as the bombs exploded.

I entered the small building where the doctor's quarters were. I could see several rooms; each had to be checked, but I could also hear the sound of music playing from one of the rooms.

I made my way towards the music, checking each room. It looked like this building had to be the officer's quarters, as each room had a single bed in it, a desk and a small wardrobe.

The rest of the rooms are empty, so I approach the last room which has the music playing. I opened the door quickly and burst in, pistol at the ready.

"Nein, Nein! Violence is not the answer!" He shouted, fearing for his life.

I could not tell Heidi, but it was always going to be the case; everyone had to die. Heidi was not going to like this at all, but I didn't give a shit if she liked the doctor. I covered the doctor and the building with fuel and made my way out.

There was one other building to check in the compound, the one where Regina was tortured and shot. I re-grouped with the others and we headed off towards the building.

"What did you do with the doctor, Petra?" asked Heidi.

"Do not worry Heidi, he has been dealt with accordingly."

"What does that even mean, Petra? Did you kill him?"

"We have to move quickly and finish this - shift your ass now!"

We ensured that the last building was clear. In one of the rooms, I found a wall plan of the camp showing the airstrip in the adjacent field.

"There is an airstrip in the next field, we must make sure no one is there before we set fire to anything girls."

"We have to get out of here, Petra," stated Heidi.

"Not until we have cleared everywhere, Heidi. No one can be left alive."

"Don't push your luck Petra, so far we have got away with this, let's just get out of here," said Heidi.

We walked through a small forest area and arrived at the clearing. I saw a small building across the other side, there was one sentry standing at the door and I saw no planes. I asked the other two girls to slowly and quietly make their way around the other side and wait for my signal. Once they were in position I walked out and towards the man. He instantly challenged me, and Hannah sprang into action and knocked him out with the butt of her rifle.

I peered through a small window and couldn't see anyone. I could see a desk, but no one was sitting at it. I opened the door quietly and crept inside. Moving slowly towards an open door, behind which I could hear voices talking about a shipment of diamonds, coming in from Africa by train via Rome. As I cleared the door, I could see a uniformed man and a woman both standing at a desk with their backs to me. Seizing the moment! I let a shot off and it hit the man in the shoulder who fell to the ground; the woman started screaming hysterically. As he fell, I could see it was Schellenberg; he went for his pistol, but he was too slow, I had him covered.

The others had entered the room by this stage and helped me secure Schellenberg. Hannah walked over to a picture that was hung on the wall of Hitler and smashed it to the ground. Spinning on my heels and heading for the guard, that had now come around, raising my pistol toward his head, he started pleading with me not to shoot him....

"Please, please, I have a family!" That simply enraged me more.

"So did I." These were the last words he heard.

Heidi was struggling to keep the secretary quiet; her screams were so loud it was hurting my ears.

"Shut her up, Heidi, or I will," I shouted over the noise.

All this time Schellenberg said nothing, just sat in a chair holding his wounded shoulder.

"Remember me?" I asked him, as I kicked his foot to get his attention.

"Suck my dick, dirty whore," he snarled at me and continued with a barrage of insults toward me.

I raised my pistol towards his groin area and smiled, then pulled the trigger, and nothing. I pulled it again, still nothing. Both times he flinched! I could see the sweat now running down his forehead. It must have been the adrenaline, I wasn't paying attention nor counting my shots.

"What's the matter with this thing," I said out loud.

"You're out of bullets, stupid bitch," Schellenberg replied. "If you're going to shoot someone, at least make sure you have enough bullets to do the job!"

Hannah hit him in the head from behind and told him to be quiet.

I took his pistol from Heidi, cocked it and took aim again.

"I might still be new to all this shooting people game, but I am a quick learner, and I don't like to be laughed at."

This time, when I pulled the trigger, I immediately saw Schellenberg holding his groin and moaning in pain. Then I saw the blood; it covered his hands and legs quickly and started to form a puddle on the floor under his chair. I allowed him to experience the pain for a short while before emptying the rest of his pistol into him, shooting him in his legs first, then his kneecaps and continued on shooting him everywhere, remembering every moment he and the Nazis had caused me pain over the past years. With every bullet, I shouted, "*Now you will pay!*"

I then turned to the secretary, remembering the conversation they were having about diamonds. "Now, what is your name?"

"M-Monika."

"Well, Monika. Here is your first and last chance to save your fucking life. I am in no mood for games, do you want to meet the same fate as your boss?" I pointed over to the blood covered, lifeless body of Schellenberg. I pulled back the hammer on my pistol and pointed it at her head. "Tell me everything you know about these diamond shipments."

"They bring them in every month from Africa by courier, he travels by boat and train because he had a plane crash some years ago and now has a fear of flying. They use them to help finance the war, the route he takes, and the dates are on Schellenberg's desk. He travels alone, always wears a black hat and gloves and walks with a limp - he lost his left leg in the crash."

"Thank you, Monika, now get what you need and leave."

As she walked towards the door, I slowly drew my pistol to her head height. I pulled the trigger and shot her in the head as we couldn't leave anyone alive to inform on us.

"What are you doing Petra?" screamed Heidi.

"What is required, Heidi, now sort your fucking self out right now."

I looked over the details on Schellenberg's desk; it showed just how complacent the Nazis had become. They sent the same man on the same date every month on the same route carrying diamonds! This intelligence was worth keeping, I thought to myself.

"Heidi, can you find something to cover these bodies please?"

"We have to get out of here Petra, before we have the whole German army surrounding us," fretted Heidi.

"Heidi, always worrying, aren't you? Calm down, don't take any notice of how Petra is talking to you right. Ignore her anger, we need to sort out our next move," stated Hannah.

"What is our next move, Petra, where are we going to go?"

"To be honest I only got as far as this, any suggestions?"

There was a long pause from all of us.

"Well, I have a contact in the French resistance; I had a relationship with him whilst I was in school. As soon as war broke out, he joined the resistance."

"Oh, the boyfriend! Thought you said he was in the military?" I asked.

"I never stated which branch, did I, Petra?"

"And you are confident you can find him, Heidi?" asked Hannah.

"Yes, for sure, no problem."

"Okay then, its settled, let's finish off here, collect anything worth any value and let's get the hell out of here."

Dowsing the place with petrol, Petra lit a match and set it ablaze.

We started making our way to France, uncertain of what sort of reception we would get.

Chapter Five

Hannah

We started walking, heading in a southerly direction towards Dresden, a town close to Czechoslovakia. The map I took from Schellenberg's desk showed a small village only five kilometres away. As we walked, I realized that we needed a change of clothing and some transportation as we couldn't travel by train or any other method that would bring us in contact with any Gestapo or German uniformed personnel as they might stop us and ask for our papers, identification and travel, none of which we had.

"We will rest here for a while, girls. We are not far from a small village. I think we should take our time getting there so we arrive at night, then under the cover of darkness we can steal some clothes and maybe a car, what do you think?"

"Yes, sounds like a good plan, Hannah, but we aren't going to kill anyone, are we?" Heidi asked as she leaned up against a tree.

"Heidi, we will do what we must," Petra replied with a determined tone. "Now let me tend to your wounds, your dressings need changing."

I watched as Petra cared for Heidi and my thoughts drifted to my burns. I could feel each and every inch of them; the rough cloth of the army shirt I was wearing felt like sandpaper, rubbing against them as I moved.

I checked the compass which we had taken from the dead guard. When I closed it and went to replace it in the bag, I noticed an inscription on the back which simply said, *so you can always find your way home*.

It must have been a gift, from a sweetheart or his wife. *War takes so much from us all and it can turn kind, loving people into monsters*, I thought to myself as I placed it back into the bag.

"Right girls, let's get moving."

As we walked, I could not help but wonder what we must look like three young women, dressed in a mish mash of male German uniforms and female clothing and wearing army boots, most of which didn't fit any of us.

We continued to walk, taking our time as we had to constantly adjust our direction to keep in the cover of hedge rows and forested areas. If any soldiers saw us, we would stand out a mile.

While taking another rest I looked at the map once again. We had less than a kilometre to go, daylight was giving way to the night sky as the stars crept into view.

"Hannah, would you like me to look at your burns?" asked Heidi. I think her nurturing instincts were taking over, she was portraying all those Mutter-like qualities. Again, my thoughts returned to her not having the strength for what the future held.

We ate some bread and fruit that we had taken from the camp. That was something else we had to steal; more food and water. Heidi and Petra then slept for an hour or two. Away from the city it was quiet in the countryside. Occasionally I heard the droning sound of an aircraft carried by the night from a distance.

It was now 2am. I woke the girls; it was time to go.

We approached the village, there were only a few homes, but it was going to be easy as no one locked their doors at night. We removed our boots and entered the first house, tip toeing around the kitchen and other rooms downstairs, thinking it was best not to go upstairs in order not to wake anyone and suffer any kind of confrontation.

The girls and I systematically and quietly moved through the village, checking every home as we went and collecting whatever we could.

We made our way down a small road with large thick hedgerows looking for a way through, finally locating a gate after about half a kilometre, clambering over it, and taking refuge behind the hedge to look at our loot.

We changed our clothes and ate some meat we had taken from one of the houses. Petra had stolen a couple of large handbags, and as we went through them and discarded everything we didn't want, we found they contained identification papers, money and some lipstick. So now we looked more like actual German women and not like half-bred soldiers. We washed some of the muck of our hands and faces using some of the fresh water and used our old clothes as towels. Although this was an improvement, Heidi, with her facial cuts and I with some of my burns still visible, would still encourage a lasting gaze from anyone we met.

Although there were several vehicles in the village none of them had any fuel in them. This was not strange as there was a shortage, due to most of it being taken by the Nazi regime.

We decided to find somewhere safe to rest for the remaining hours prior to dawn breaking.

In the morning and with the light of day we looked more closely at the papers Petra had stolen. One set was for an elderly lady of about sixty years old - well that wasn't going to work at all as we were all about the same age, around twenty years old. The other set was for a thirty-year old female; with a little more make-up, one of us could pass for her.

We had plenty of money which we'd stolen from the dead soldiers and from the houses in the village. We decided we would chance using the buses from village to village or town, keeping away from the major cities as we were more likely to be stopped and checked there.

For the next couple of days, we zig zagged our way south east by bus. I was right though, Heidi and myself were on the receiving end of many a long stare, and some people even asked Heidi what had happened. She told them the truth; that she had been caught up in the bombing of Berlin and was heading south to escape it. They bought it, mostly remarking *"poor girl, I don't blame you."* We were not the only ones trying to escape the horror, many people had fled to the countryside.

As we travelled, I could see that the war was beginning to leave its mark everywhere. Downed burnt out or burning planes, large craters were everywhere, left by British bombing crews who had missed their targets by miles I presumed, as I could not see anything worth bombing around here. So many buildings in ruins and families left without homes. The Nazi regime had believed so strongly that Germany would never be bombed. They couldn't have got it more wrong; the actual reality of war was everywhere for everyone to see.

We finally reached the town of Bamberg, which was about forty-five kilometres north of Nuremberg. Petra suggested we get rooms there and clean up, so we found somewhere to stay overnight. The rooms are basic in nature, a bed, a small dark oak bedside table and a lamp. The curtains are very thin, something we are not used to coming from a city, I guess they don't follow blackout protocol in the smaller towns.

I noticed that the town seemed as though it had not yet suffered from the war, apart from the rationing imposed across the country of several food items and fuel. There was a small number of soldiers about, but they were young men on leave visiting their families. Of course, the unmistakable flags of the Nazi party hung everywhere, which only served to fuel my growing mistrust of the regime. These flags now represented everything I disliked about this so-called master race!

Petra and Heidi came to my room and we sat for a while discussing our next move.

"We are going to need more papers; one set isn't going to get us very far," stated Petra.

"I stick out, Hannah, and would only draw attention to us." Heidi was of course right. Her bandages did certainly stand out.

"Okay, Petra and I will have a wander around and see what we can find with regards to papers. Heidi, you get us packed and ready to move. Okay?"

"Okay, Hannah."

As Petra and I walked around the town, we noticed plenty of women around our age so you'd think it would be easy to steal handbags, but it seemed everyone in this town had become cautious and very attached to what they have. They clutched their bags in front of them, they placed them on tables in front of them, they never took their eyes off them!

We sat in a café watching for several hours, discussing our options.

"Petra, I think the only way to get what we need is to kill someone; we follow them home and take what we need."

"Whatever it takes Hannah, doesn't make any fucking difference to me."

We continued to watch the people going about their evening. We needed someone of similar age and hair colour to our own.

Another hour passed and just as we were about to give up, I spotted a girl walking alone with brunette hair like Petra's. We followed her home, keeping our distance. She was also about the same build to us so, we could also acquire fresh clothing.

"Right, we give her thirty minutes to settle in and then we go," I whispered to Petra.

Giving her the allotted time, I pulled my knife in readiness and grabbed Petra's arm. "Right, let's go!"

Suddenly, there was a voice from the shadows. "Hold it, don't move." A soft male voice said from the shadows.

A man moved slowly out from where he had been watching us with a pistol pointed toward us.

"Weapons, please," he ordered.

We handed over our pistols and the knife I had. I could feel myself shaking. *Shit, Gestapo*, I thought to myself, as he was dressed just like one in a trench coat and hat. Petra didn't say a word.

"Right let's go, ladies, slowly and quietly if you please."

"Who are you, what do want?" I asked him.

"Hands in pockets, ladies, and stay quiet."

He led us to a café and told us to sit, keeping his hand in his pocket hiding his pistol. I knew at this point he was not Gestapo. If he was, then he would have no issue holding us at gunpoint in plain view, with a couple of guards standing watch over us.

"Sit, and remember stay quiet, not a word."

It was getting late and the streets are almost empty, the café was preparing to close, but he ordered some drinks.

"Who are you?" I asked again.

He just stared back at me, shifting his gaze from me to Petra. The waitress brought the drinks and then continued her chores, cleaning tables and preparing the place to close.

"Who are you?" I snarled. "I know you're not Gestapo, for if you were, we would not be talking in a café, we would both be locked up in some dirty room somewhere that no one has ever heard of and brutally tortured. But I know that's not what you want. Is it money you're after?"

"Oh, you're right about one thing, I am not Gestapo or even German military. And no, I don't want money. Let me tell you what I know."

"Back in 1938, a lady called Kitty Schmitt was approached by Schellenberg and Heydrich to run a top-secret operation out of her brothel. The Nazis took prostitutes from the streets, trained them in many aspects of espionage and then placed them in the brothel. Their objective was mainly to gather intelligence from ranking officers and civilians."

"Who the fuck are you?" Petra barked.

"All in good time," he replied, and continued, "then the British started bombing Berlin and the brothel was razed to the ground, killing almost everyone. Several of you survived the bombing, only to be rescued by Schellenberg and taken back to the training camp where it all started.

We are not too sure what happened at the camp - the next time we heard about the three of you, you were heading south. For what reason only you know, but you stole the clothes you're wearing from a small village, took several buses, and now here we are."

"Who are you and how do you know all this?" I asked again, in what could only be describe as a worried tone.

He continued, "The Nazis were recording everything that was said in the brothel. What they didn't know was that we were recording them, as well as keeping them under surveillance. We knew some of you were still alive well before they did; we could hear you moaning in the rubble. One of the radios was still transmitting for several hours after the bombing."

"You're an agent? From where? The French resistance?" I asked, but I was not getting any reply from him.

"I will tell you everything you need to know but not here, we must get moving."

"What about our friend Heidi, we can't leave her." Petra asked as we stood up.

"She is already with my colleague at a safe location. Follow me."

"Where the fuck is he taking us, Hannah?" asked Petra as we followed the man to a nearby car.

"I am not sure, Petra, but let's keep an open mind for now. They have Heidi so we have no choice but to go along with him for the time been, okay?"

"Okay, Hannah."

We drove for what seemed to be hours through the darkness, occasionally driving through a town or city which strangely enough didn't seem to have any bomb damage. I realised we were no longer in Germany, that was for sure.

"Who are you?" I asked again.

"I am with British Intelligence, Hannah. Don't worry, you're safe and so is your friend. Try and get some sleep."

That was all I was going to get out of him for now, so I closed my eyes and felt myself drifting in and out but not sleeping really. Why would I, who was this person? Where was he taking us?

Dawn was breaking when we arrived at a mountain cabin.

"Where are we?"

"Austrian mountains, at a British safe house," he replied. "Okay, so from this moment forward you can call me 'Falcon' and this is 'Viper'."

"Hannah, I've been so worried, she brought me here at gunpoint and wouldn't tell me anything." An incredibly happy Heidi hugged me as though she would never let go.

"Steady, Heidi!"

"Oh, sorry Hannah I forgot, I am just so pleased to see you."

Heidi grabbed Petra as though she was a long-lost sister and hugged her so tightly, she almost broke her ribs.

"Holy shit Heidi, it's good to see you too."

"Who are these people, Hannah? And what do they want with us?" Heidi asked, standing between Petra and I as though it made her feel safer.

"It's okay Heidi, they work for the British."

"You're probably wondering why you're here?" asks Falcon.

"Yes, there are many questions racing through my head right now."

"Hannah, I said I would tell you everything you wanted to know, and I will, firstly let me explain why you're here," replied Falcon, whilst taking a seat at the table in the middle of the room. "Please sit, have some coffee."

"So, you know we have had you under surveillance for months now, and from your actions we know you have no love for the Nazis, that is for certain, although you Hannah did have. I will cut the normal crap out and get straight to it."

"Viper and I have been operating in occupied territory since the war broke out. Our main job is to find and train resistance fighters but generally single self-confident individuals to work on their own and on occasions with other larger groups to cause as much disruption and chaos as they can, hit and run tactics kind of stuff. Shall I continue?"

"You have my attention," I replied as I looked at the other two girls, who simply gave a slight nod of approval.

"As I said, we have been observing you ever since you entered the training camp. Therefore, we know you already have a certain amount of training. We have been authorised to offer you all the chance to be trained and then work for the British government as our agents."

"What would we get in return?" I asked.

"Everything you need to succeed; new identity papers, money, a place to live, clothing, training," Falcon replied.

"And if we refuse?"

"Then you can go back to fumbling around in the dark, stealing and murdering your own people to get by. Honestly, how long do you think you would last or get away with that?"

"We will need some time to discuss it."

"Alright. We have to be going; we will return tomorrow and expect an answer by then," Falcon stated, as they got up and headed for the door. They left the cabin and we sat for a while in silence, each of us contemplating our future, but one thing kept coming to the front of my mind. Diamonds.

"Look girls, we have been lucky so far; the way I see it we can either continue on with what we have and try to get the diamonds, or we can take up his offer. They will provide us with new papers and other things we need; we let them train us and then go for the diamonds at some later date. After all, the courier travels the same route around the same date every month. We certainly shouldn't trust them, and why should we, but we can use them for what we want and need right now!"

"But Hannah, we have just got free of one controlling factor in our lives, now you're suggesting we enter another?" replied Petra as she poured herself another coffee.

"What do you think Heidi?" I asked

"I thought we were going to attach ourselves to the French resistance, then sort out how to get the diamonds and get out of all this. You know I am not like you two, I don't like the killing, Hannah."

"You think we fucking liked it, Heidi? It just has to be done sometimes. Falcon was right about one thing; if we refuse, we will certainly have to continue struggling on alone," stated Petra.

"Personally speaking, I think it's a good move. After a few months we will be better trained and more capable, we'll have new papers and somewhere to live; it gives us a much better chance of success. I say we do it; after all we are already killing Germans, why not make it easier for ourselves and get something out of it?"

"Petra, come on, you know it makes sense, yes we don't trust them, but that doesn't mean we can't use them!"

She didn't reply; both Petra and Heidi sat in silence mulling over my comments, I hoped. At this stage I had made my mind up anyway, but they have their own minds, we all have to make our own path in life. I left them to their thoughts and went for some fresh air.

At this stage I actually felt at ease with my new direction and the thought of becoming more effective and proficient left me with a warm glow. It was so peaceful up here in the mountains, birds singing going about their daily routines and the breeze hitting my face was cooling and soothing to my skin. I lifted my blouse to allow it to flow under onto my burns. For the first time in days - months actually - I felt a calming feeling come over me. The woodlands were alive with all the forest creatures that made this place their home, completely unaware of the horrific world they now resided in.

I sat and closed my eyes and filled my ears with the bird songs around me. It wasn't long before I found myself transported back to my childhood, playing with my friends or simply sitting with my Mutter in our garden, embracing nature as it went about providing life to an array of creatures. A hand softly touched my shoulder, I opened one eye and saw Petra move in front of me and sit by my side.

"Hannah, it's nice to see you smile, what are you thinking about?"

"My family, my friends. I was just remembering how things used to be at home, and this place reminds me of that."

"You were born and raised in a place like this?"

"Umm, not quite, no, but in the countryside with rolling hills, not mountains like these."

"Isn't it strange, Hannah, one minute you're going through hell, bombs dropping all around you, fighting for your life and the next you're sat somewhere like this, quiet apart from nature going about its business."

"I could live here forever, Petra."

"You like this kind of scenery, Hannah? I long for the city again, I miss the city, I loved going the cinema with my parents, eating and drinking in cafés, walking through the park." Petra recalls.

"I miss my parents so much; it hurts every time I think about them." I replied

"Yes Hannah I agree, I don't know if that ever goes away; I use to think been in the city, Berlin, in some way kept me closer to them."

"I guess that's what makes us all the same but different at the same time, Petra, we all lose people that is for sure in life, but how we remember them is different."

"Maybe you're right Hannah, but for now, our paths are entwined. You both have your reasons and I have mine for doing what we are doing. One thing I do find myself missing from time to time is the touch of a man, even those that paid me for it. Isn't that strange considering what we used to do?"

"Maybe a little, yes. As for me, I have had my fill of men for now, anyway can you ever see any man wanting to get close to a body like mine!"

"As for the future, Petra, have you decided what you're going to do?"

"Yes, I am going to take them up on their offer."

"Glad to hear it; I am too. What do you think Heidi will do?"

"Honestly, I don't know, Hannah, she has lost all her confidence due to the cuts on her face. She feels ugly and is suffering with her thoughts."

"Yes, I have seen the look on her face when she gazes into a mirror, she no longer likes what she sees."

"She might feel better once her cuts heal," Petra replies, and headed inside to check on Heidi.

I spent the rest of the afternoon sat in the sunshine, taking in my surroundings and forgetting the war for a while. As we were preparing some food that evening Heidi was quiet, not really saying much of anything. She had withdrawn completely.

I broke the silence. "What are you thinking about Heidi?"

"I am not sure I can do this Hannah. Look at me, I stick out like you wouldn't believe, what good could I be?"

"You are thinking about the here and now Heidi, it will take time to train us. Maybe not as much as someone starting from scratch with no basic training, but time, nonetheless. By then your cuts will have healed and you can hide most of them with makeup."

"You don't have to do this Heidi," replied Petra.

"It's entirely your choice, no one is forcing you to do anything anymore Heidi. If you decide you're staying, then Petra and I will help you through it."

We ate and went to sleep—well the other girls did, I had intermittent moments of what I thought was sleep. I think the main issue was not knowing what Heidi was going to do. Petra and I worried about her, even when she was close by, my burns are also catching on my clothes still, they are healing and starting to itch like crazy; it's starting to drive me mad!

The morning seemed to come quite quickly and once again Petra and I had to endure the silence from Heidi as she continued to contemplate our situation. We didn't have long to wait though; Falcon and Viper had returned as agreed.

"Morning ladies," Falcon said as he walked through the door in a rather chirpy voice with Viper not far behind him.

"So, what's it going to be?" Viper asked. She wasn't one for small talk.

"Petra and I are in. Heidi what are you going to do?"

"Okay, okay, um..."

"You in or out, Heidi?" Viper pushed for an answer, which I thought at the time was possibly not the best tactic.

"Yes, okay I'm in!" Heidi replied in a loud voice with a concerned look on her face.

"That's great, your training will start in a little while. Firstly, let's talk about what we actually do, but first, let's have a cup of coffee." said Falcon.

Chapter Six

Objectives & Training

Falcon

"Our primary objective is to cause as much disruption to the enemy as possible using whatever means necessary, including but not limited to, sabotage, intelligence gathering and killing when required. We operate only behind enemy lines. Any questions so far?"

"No, not yet," we all responded.

Falcon resumed, "This training normally takes several months. However, due to you already having gone through some experience from the Nazis we can skip through large parts, but you will be tested on every aspect of the program just to be sure. If you pass, it will dramatically reduce the time it will take you to become operational."

"The first thing we are going to test are your abilities and see if there are any obvious weak spots. Follow me." Viper gestured with her hand.

We went outside and followed Viper to their car. She opened the boot and there we saw an array of weapons, pistols, rifles and shotguns.

"Take a pistol each and load it," she instructed us.

Falcon had set up some targets for us to shoot at whilst we were with Viper at the car.

"Right, ladies, let's see what you've got," he said, moving away from the targets of old cans and bottles resting on a large log.

Our former small arms training was extensive; the Germans had made us use a Mauser HSC pistol. It was a small but powerful pistol, and easy to conceal for a woman. This part was easy for all three of us, each taking a turn and not missing anything we aimed at. For the rest of the day both Falcon and Viper took it in turns to test our abilities on map reading, unarmed combat and basic communications, all of which was straightforward but I guess they had to find out what we could do.

The next day our training started early, 05.30 in fact. This was our first fail; Falcon and Viper tested our alertness which was zero as we all had red marks on our necks imitating a kill.

"You are all dead! Today and from this moment forward you will learn to be alert at all times day and night," shouted Viper.

"Personal security and that of your fellow agents must at all times be at the forefront of your mind! How is this achieved? By following some simple guidelines, information is the key factor here!"

Security training

1. Local conditions – your surroundings, your room, the building you're in, the streets around the building, key points such as bus and train stations, police and forces buildings, everything of importance that can or might affect you.

2. Local regulations – are there any kind of regulations imposed on a daily basis, black outs, curfew, ID checks and the like.

3. Enemy personnel and methods – their current positions and strength, every aspect of weapons, vehicle and buildings used.

4. Your own people – always be aware of where your subordinates are and what they are doing.

5. When sleeping, place a chair against the door, under the handle to prevent access.

"These are just some of the foundations for good security, it is something that must become second nature which requires self-discipline and continued self-training and awareness on a daily basis. You must know everything there is to know about your surroundings and those around you."

At this point I couldn't help but wonder how the hell we had managed to get this far and get away with so much. The three of us from that moment forward started quizzing each other about the cabin and the surrounding area, every inch was to be imprinted in our minds.

Communication training – what you say or write down can give you away, loose lips sink ships.

"Some of the things you should never do are as follows," stated Falcon.

1. Never talk about anything related to your job in a public place or on the phone.

2. Never write anything down that could compromise you in any way, memorise everything, burn any documents that you no longer need.

3. Your behaviour. Try at all times to blend in, your clothing, your actions, drinking and eating, you need to become an average citizen.

4. Have a solid cover story: why you are there, who knows you.

5. Never use the same café on a regular basis, look out for familiar faces, are they following you?

"When choosing accommodation there are certain factors which much be considered."

1. Can you get in and out without raising suspicion from neighbours and passers-by?

2. You must have a genuine reason for frequent visits.

3. Whenever possible choose isolated buildings, cabins, farm buildings; the more isolated the better. Make sure they have several entrances and exit points.

4. Always have someone on sentry duty at all time whilst in these situations.

It soon became noticeably clear to Petra and myself that this kind of stuff was Heidi's forte. She was like a sponge and she certainly kept both of us in full alertness mode. Finally, Heidi had something to occupy her mind and divert it away from her facial cuts.

Each part of a machine must play its part, otherwise it fails, and Heidi had found hers: security and communications. For the next few days, we practiced until we all knew every item and every inch of our surrounding; we had even managed to have an escape plan on standby.

At night, we each took our turn at sentry duty. We had positioned trip wires in the woodland to warn us of approaching individuals, we quizzed each other on Falcon and Viper's clothes on each day, their faces, and their mannerisms until we knew every inch of them.

Cover story training – this must be as realistic as possible to hide your true purpose. Have solid links from the past to the present and ensure all your papers are in order for your cover story.

"Here there are several points that must at all times be considered," Viper explained whilst pouring a coffee.

1. You must have a plausible story.

2. Solid links to your actual past, whenever possible.

3. Your most recent history is usually of particular interest to police or check points.

If it wasn't for our current surroundings, I would have thought I was back at the Nazi school for girls. I was beginning to have information overload and needed a break for a while from the constant influx of new material.

This wasn't to be though; even when Falcon and Viper had left for the day, we then had Heidi constantly at us, questioning and quizzing us. It was good as we needed to know our stuff, because it just might save our lives one day.

"Are they expecting us to return to getting fucked several times a day then, Hannah?" Petra asked the question that was running through my mind too.

"Umm, that isn't going to work for myself or Heidi is it, Petra?" I said, pointing to Heidi's face and my burns. "They are not stupid and can clearly see that, I am sure."

"That might be the case for you two, but I am definitely not going back to that shitty life. What is our cover story going to be if it's supposed to link to our past?"

"We are going to have to come up with something before they do," I replied in a concerned tone. I honestly couldn't see any kind of scenario were returning to prostitution wouldn't work for Heidi or myself, and although our scars will get better given time, they would result in neither of us being desirable to any man.

The sense of conflict stirred within each of us regarding this particular issue as we each had our own reasons for not wanting to return to that life again.

"I don't mind men; in fact, I enjoy their company, but not as a prostitute," Petra chipped in.

"You still have your looks, Petra, and a great body, I am sure you will find someone to help fill those needs, at least one of us still has that opportunity," Heidi said sarcastically.

"Oh, Heidi there was no fucking need for that; you know what I meant, and I wasn't making any references to either of you."

"You two, stop the bitching right now, I get we are all becoming frustrated and it's starting to cause us to fall out with each other. We each have different wants and needs, let's not fall out over them." Tempers were starting to fray, and I had to put some distance between them. "Petra, go walk it off."

The next day I spoke to Falcon regarding getting out of here for a few hours and it was agreed that either he or Viper would take us one at a time into one of the nearby villages, starting that day with Petra.

"Petra, you come with me," stated Viper, continuing, "You two have a practical test-day ahead of you with Falcon."

Heidi and I spent most of the day being tested by Falcon over the past few days' material and I was surprised just how much I had retained, but I guess that was thanks to Heidi constantly practicing with us.

During a moment's break I sat with Falcon and we talked about him for a while. "How long have you been with the SOE?" I asked.

"For a little over two years now. I was sent to Canada, and like you I was trained in all aspects of espionage, sabotage techniques, subversion, intelligence gathering, lock picking, explosives training, radio communication, encoding/decoding, recruiting and the art of silent killing with a large side order of unarmed combat. It was interesting, and this is what we will be training you in. In our work you have to be ready for anything; you should be able to adapt in certain situations."

"Is there any part of the training you really enjoyed? You know, like us, Heidi with the technological stuff, Petra with the silent killing, and of course me, target practice."

"Of course, Hannah, I think everyone finds some part of the training that they really excel in. For me, it was explosives, I really like finding different items to hide them in, as well as the several types, just about everything to do with them."

"There are different types?"

"Yes, distinct types for different uses - take a normal hand grenade, you can throw it, you can use it to set a trap."

"Really? How do you set a trap with a hand grenade? Once you have pulled the pin doesn't it explode?"

"Pull the pin, but do not release the lever, hold it down, because it only becomes live once the lever is released. Now place it under someone you have just killed, using the body weight to keep the lever in place. Anyone now rolling the body over with spring the trap. BOOM!"

"That is both clever and sneaky; I like that!"

Petra and Viper returned late that afternoon.

"How was your day, Petra?" Hannah asked.

"We sat in cafés and walked around, and all the time she was questioning me about our surroundings and the people in it. I thought it was going to be a few hours of relaxation, but these people never fucking stop."

"It's been the same here, nonstop. Even whilst we had a break, I was taught something new, but at least you got away from here for a while."

"The change of scenery was good, yes. Viper isn't very approachable you know, she doesn't like talking much, funny bitch."

"Maybe that's just the training. Remember, only tell people what they need to know."

"True, very true Hannah."

The training continued the next day.

Interrogation methods

Viper explained, "If you are stopped by either the police or general check points, they will ask you four questions in most cases and you should always have the answers ready and reply with confidence."

1. Who are you?

2. Where do you come from?

3. What papers do you have?

4. What are you doing?

"If you fail to satisfy the individual in a general stop or check then you most likely will be arrested and sent for further interrogation by specially trained staff; the Gestapo!"

I for one failed this training at the first hurdle; they placed a black hood over my head, dragged me around to totally disorientate me, strapped me a chair and I knew they were going to leave me there for days. No food or water, they wouldn't let me sleep. I gave up within hours, the whole experience was too much.

Petra, on the other hand, seemed to like it, but then I always thought she didn't mind the rough stuff - after all she came from the streets. Heidi was the one that surprised the hell out of us both, she managed to last the longest. Where that came from, Petra and I would never know.

Anyway, the other girls helped me practice and after several more sessions I manage to last the two days.

"Some of the general techniques used by these people may include some of the following:

- Bright lights facing you.
- Hanging from the ceiling.
- Seated but uncomfortable, no water or food.
- Exhaustion, extended periods without sleep.

"Trick questioning may also be used so be aware of this."

- Lengthy periods of silence intended to procure unsolicited remarks.
- Differing methods of approach referring to the same question.
- Exaggeration of your participation in a particular event.
- Suggestions you are alone, abandoned by colleagues.
- False confessions by colleagues.
- Intimidation using a firing squad or other methods.
- Threats to family and friends

"Some things you need to be aware of prior to interrogation:

- If placed in a prison cell, there may be hidden microphones, stool pigeons, one-way mirrors or over friendly staff; say nothing!

"During your interrogation you must try to follow these simple rules:

- Speak slowly, be clear and firm, don't answer simple questions immediately.
- Do not be abusive.
- Crying will not impress anyone.
- Always reply with a closed answer.
- Deny everything you can't explain plausibly.
- Never express feelings for anyone.

"Remember, the Gestapo has built a reputation on ruthlessness, not on intelligence. They will use every trick in the book in an attempt to ply information out of you or get you to admit something. Stay calm and rely on your back story."

Target selection

"For the most part, your missions or objectives will come directly from London through one of us. Falcon will explain the basics."

"Any operation relies on facts for success, which can be broken down into three simple steps."

1. Information – regarding your target, everything you can find out about, area, personnel, entry and exit points, your people. The more information you have the better chance of success.

2. Intention – sabotage, burglary, intelligence gathering, target acquisition and taking out. Again, this needs to be decided and planned out down to the last detail.

3. Method – how will you proceed; what materials are required and what backup plan do you have in case of failure?

"Every detail must be covered, if you have to put pen to paper, then destroy it as soon as you can."

This was of particular interest to me as it was going to be used sooner than they thought, but for personal reasons that I didn't want to share with them, and I was so pleased the other two hadn't mentioned it either.

Over the next few days, we continued to practice until everything became second nature. We did skip many of the usual training programs due to our prior training. In fact, one particular part was detailed background information on the Nazi party; it was agreed we probably knew far more about that than most agents due to our backgrounds.

One thing I found interesting was the British use of everyday items to hide weapons and information or other useful tools. Viper arrived one day with some of these items which we all had some fun with for a while - handbags with a concealed knife, lipstick with a small compass concealed in it and a ring with poison. I did begin to consider the fact that we were being prepared and trained for things we could never imagine.

The ring, a new and special piece of kit from the British SOE, looked like a really nice piece of jewellery, but in fact it was a deadly, silent kill weapon. A ring with a light blue stone, pop off top which reveals a small spike. Simply scratch or prick someone with it and a deadly toxic venom is injected into them. The venom is so strong it will disable any person within seconds and kill them in under a minute. Neurotoxin Tetrodotoxin was a venom taken from the **Blue Ring Octopus** with no antivenom available, so we had to be careful with it. There was also no method available for anyone to trace it in the human body. The venom was loaded on the underside of the ring via a small one-way hole, using a syringe. Once loaded, pop the top off and it's primed, ready for use. It could only be used if within striking distance, so close quarter contact was required.

After several weeks of training and practicing our new skills with regular tests from both Falcon and Viper it was considered we were ready, mission ready! Only one thing remained, our cover stories.

Heidi's facial scars had healed quite well. However, a couple of the scars were still visible even under makeup. As for my burn scars, I could cover them using the right clothing, and wearing my hair down and forward hid the scars on my neck.

This was actually the part none of us was looking forward to; The cover story, even talking about it brought on feelings of anxiety but now was the right time to sort this out. Falcon and Viper needed to sort out our new papers and other documentation which would be provided by London.

"Morning, ladies, today is a day on which we have to decide a few things. Firstly, where you will reside and operate, your cover stories and how long it will take before you are settled and ready for operations." Falcon seemed far too excited about this for my liking.

"What do you think?" Hannah asked him.

"It's simple, why try and invent something when you already have a fully plausible story?"

"So, you want us to go back into prostitution then?"

"Is that not what you did?" Viper chipped in.

"Yes, but we wanted to leave that all behind us. Anyway, look at me, no one will want this body once I uncover it. How do you expect me to work looking like this?"

"Every brothel has a structure Hannah, a madam, someone in charge."

"This was your plan from the beginning, wasn't it?"

"Look, instead of working for someone else you will be in charge, you can run your own brothel, so you're not exactly returning to prostitution in the real sense. It's a perfect cover, it can be a reliable source of information and it's something you're all totally familiar with. It's the perfect cover."

I could see the anger rising in Petra 1from that remark and I am sure she thought about going over to Viper and giving her a slap, but maybe thought better of it.

"We need some time to consider this - you will have to give us some time."

They both walked out and the cabin fell into total silence. This really wasn't what any of us wanted to ever do again, but Falcon was probably right. It was the perfect cover story for all three of us and it meant we could continue to work together.

"Options, ladies. Heidi, you have gone incredibly quiet again."

"We can run," replied Heidi.

"How far do you think we will get, Heidi? We hardly have any money and the British have agents all over the place."

"I don't want to go back to that life," remarked Heidi, as she sat at the table with her head down on her arms.

"Petra?"

"This was their plan from the fucking start. They are just as bad as the Nazis, manipulating and controlling. The way I see it, we don't have a lot of choice now, we have put so much into this, but again I want to make it clear, I don't fucking trust them!"

"All good points, girls, maybe we have jumped out of the pan and into the fire. I say we try and make the best of it."

"How do you mean Hannah?" asked Heidi.

"We ask for something in return. I don't know about you girls, but I want something to look forward to, a future, so we make sure we can build one!"

"Yeah, the diamonds, Hannah?" asked Petra.

"Yes, and any other possibilities that might arise from the situation. If we are going to do this, let's make as much money out of it as possible."

"Okay, so what do you have in mind?" Heidi asked with a muffled voice from her face down position.

"The British supply everything we need to set up - money, documents, everything and we also get to keep anything we steal from the Nazis."

The rest of the day we ran through some possible cities of operation; we certainly didn't want to return to Berlin. Falcon had already ruled that out as there wasn't much of Berlin left now.

We decided on Nuremberg due to the central location. The Nazis held all their major rallies there and it was where their headquarters are, so plenty of clients with possible loose lips. As a bonus, the British had not yet targeted this city for bombing.

Now we had that sorted out we got some sleep. I hadn't had much sleep as I had all manner of things running through my head. The morning seemed to come around very quickly.

Falcon arrived alone this morning. I guess it only took one of them to find out which path we had decided to take.

"Morning, ladies, no time for pleasantries this morning, as I have other things to do, so where do we stand?"

"We will return to our old profession."

"Right, I can get London onto that straight away," he replied whilst pouring a coffee.

"We also require the ability to steal and keep for ourselves anything we like from the Germans?"

"Um...not so easy, unauthorised missions of any kind are classed as unsanctioned and are not allowed - London would go mad!"

"You picked us. We want to make sure that when the dust settles, we have a future, that's the deal or you might as well shoot us here!"

"You ladies certainly know how to drive a hard bargain. Having a fully operational circuit in the heart of the Nazi party could pay off well but it will be extremely dangerous for you." I could hear him wavering and I knew he would agree to our terms.

"Right! I will sort out the required paperwork," stated Falcon.

"How long before we have to leave?" I asked.

"It will take a few days for the paperwork, so just relax and you will be contacted when it is ready."

The next few days seemed empty as we just sat about, I did some drawings, we took walks in the woods, ate and slept but I couldn't help but think this was merely the calm before the storm. On the fourth day, Falcon finally returned with a package; it was our new papers, work permits and building ownership documents with all the required papers for working as a brothel.

One of the many things I had learnt during my school days was that the Nazis saw women as no threat. They seemed to have the impression that our only requirement in life was to provide pure Aryan babies and look after our men. This worked to our advantage; now we are *mission ready*! Well physically anyway - we are all filled with trepidation about the forthcoming months.

Chapter Seven

Hannah

Just on the outskirts of Nuremberg we came across a checkpoint. This would be our first clear test of our new papers. I drew up behind the last vehicle in a queue of three vehicles. I could feel the panic setting in, I was shaking, and I am sure if it wasn't a very warm sunny day, my sweat would certainly have given the game away. Pretty soon it was our turn, and I got control on myself by thinking about all the times we had lied to men at the brothel in Berlin. A lie is a lie.

"Halt! Papers, please," said a guard. I handed over our papers and waited patiently as the guard went through them one at a time.

"Where are you from?" the guard asked.

"We are from Neustrelitz," I continued with, "We are coming to Nuremberg for work, to open a brothel, authorized by Berlin." I handed the guard our work permits and papers.

"Umm prostitutes hey?" he asked.

"Yes," I replied. "Please come and visit us in a week's time once we are set up and open, the first night will be free."

"I see you are from Berlin, why have you not returned there?"

"We survived several of the British bombing raids but not without injury." I showed him some of my burns on my leg and neck, and Heidi reluctantly showed him some of her scars. "We wanted a fresh start and decided it was safer down here in Nuremberg, we only just got out alive!"

"Thank you, move along," the guard said, handing all the papers back to me, and I drove off slowly whilst girls smiling and waving back at the guards.

"That was intense! I was shaking the whole time, and still am," Heidi said from the back seat.

"Yes. But it was a good first test, I think we handled that quite well, girls," I replied.

Now to find our new home. None of us had been to Nuremberg before. It was quite a big city. We drove past the major Nazi party rally grounds; it was massive and although bombed by the allies back in 1940 there weren't any remaining signs of it now. They had rebuilt it very quickly.

"How many people do you think it holds?" asked Petra as she looked across the huge open expanse.

"I really couldn't say, Petra, but thousands, I think." It was an impressive place, I thought to myself as I drove past it.

Another hour past has we drove around the never-ending streets, until we finally found the building that was to be our new home. It was a small hotel, just on the outskirts of the city centre, draped in large Nazi flags like most of the buildings here due to the city's symbolic importance to the Nazi party.

I suggested we first get all our possessions inside and then we would take a look around the place and see what we needed. We had ten bedrooms in total, a lounge and bar area which was a decent size.

We were going to need some more girls. I decided five would be a good start, and at the same time as trawling the streets for them we could survey our surroundings fully. We spilt up and headed off in different directions after arranging to meet back at the brothel in two hours.

In a city this big, it was not long before I had come across a young brown-haired girl, around twenty-three years old.

"Hello, my name is Hannah. How long have you been working the streets here?"

"Three years," she replied.

"It must be hard; do you have a place to stay?"

"No, only the streets, I do everything on the streets."

"I bet it's even harder during the winter?"

"I almost didn't survive the last one, I was so ill most of the time," she replied.

"How would you like to have a place to live and work or do you prefer the streets?" I asked.

"I have a job, and I keep everything I earn," she replied.

"Look, just come and visit us tomorrow and take a look, see if you like the idea."

"Maybe," was all I got from her.

I gave her the address and thought to myself that this was not going to be as easy I had first thought. Finding the girls on the streets was easy but getting them to trust and work in a brothel was a different matter altogether. I wondered if the other two were having better luck.

I hit the same hurdles with every other girl I came across; they were distant, untrusting and some of them smelt like they had not bathed for months. I was tired and hungry, so I headed back to the brothel.

Heidi and Petra had already returned by the time I got back. It was the same for them, we would have to see what happened in the morning - if anyone turned up, that is.

The next morning, I was up and about quite early. I decided I would prepare some of the room's downstairs, cleaning and wiping everything down with a little moving around of the furniture to make it feel a little more inviting. The last owners actually must have left in a big hurry as they left basically everything behind. All the bedrooms had the beds made with clean linen, it has a fully equipped kitchen, everything a hotel needed to function is here. The only thing we have to do is stock up with some essentials of our trade, booze and condoms.

Suddenly the front door opened with a loud bang, and so, I went to see who it was.

"Good morning, Fraulein," said a black-uniformed man, giving a Nazi salute, flanked either side by soldiers. "I noticed you didn't have a flag flying outside, so I brought you a gift, my men will hang it for you."

I was pleased I didn't have to touch that flag; the very thought repulsed me. It is bad enough having to look at the pictures of Hitler hanging all over the place. The local Gestapo have clearly decided to pay us the first of many visits, no doubt.

"Papers, please." I handed mine over and called to the others to do the same who were still in their rooms upstairs. They did not respond. I was just about to go upstairs and get them when one of them shouted.

"No, no!" he pointed a pistol at me. I stopped immediately and one of them passed me at the bottom of the stairs and hurriedly went up. I could hear him shouting as he opened every door.

"Come with me, quickly," he continued to shout.

Only moments later, Heidi and Petra stood next to me in the reception area as the men rigorously checked all our papers, including our ration books. They left nothing to chance. After five minutes or so, he handed all the papers back, looked over each of us again, rolled his eyes and walked out.

"Holy crap Hannah, who was that?" asked Heidi.

"Local Gestapo as you could tell by his uniform, but they never gave any names."

"I don't like it when they say nothing, it gives me the chills," Heidi commented with a shudder.

"It's the same for all of us I think, Heidi."

Petra just walked off to get dressed.

Around eleven am there was a knock at the door, and finally four girls had turned up to check us out.

"Morning, my name is Hannah, I am the owner. Come in, ladies, and I will give you a tour."

As we walked around, I informed them of the structure. Heidi ran the bar whilst Petra was in charge of the girls and the house percentage, which was 35%.

"That sounds reasonable," one of them remarked.

"Currently you're living and working on the streets, you're open to disease, the weather and an uncertain future with no protection from anyone or anything for that matter," I replied as we entered the bar area.

"What are you offering for your 35%?" another asked.

"You will get your own room, food and clothing, security from belonging to a salon and regular bathing and health checks, oh and two days off a week. Other salons in this area would charge you much more for what I am offering you, it's a good deal and you should consider it carefully."

"It's not for me." One of them replied and walked out.

"I for one am sick of the streets, it's cold and dirty, I am in."

That was the first one, then another and another. Now we have three girls. This now provided some much-needed benefits - contact with the black market in the area for one, which we would certainly be using. All the new girls needed cleaning up, a bath and new clothing, but then none of the girls have any working attire and let's face it a brothel working girls need the right gear to highlight their best-selling points...

We got them cleaned up and let them borrow some clothes. We all then went off with our ration cards to collect what we could; we went in pairs and each of us requested an introduction to anyone they knew who had any contacts with the black market in the area. I got to meet a lady who sold her home-made biscuits from her back door and a farmer who could provide a good supply of milk. Petra went off into the northern district, where she was introduced to a soldier who could supply a few bottles of wine a month. Black markets in times of war are the life bread for some people. If you had something to trade or cash you could easily find what you wanted - providing you had someone to introduce you first.

Now loaded with several bags of cloth and clothing, we headed back to the salon. Once there we got to work altering and making the required clothing, they all needed. Ration cards would only get you some basic things; special clothing would have to be handmade. It took a couple of days or so to get everything ready but finally we were almost ready to open for business. There was just one thing that I and the other girls needed to prepare the new girls for.

"Each client will of course pay for their time with you and any alcohol they consume, but we need them to be quite drunk, then as they sleep it off take a little cash from them and hide it away in the room somewhere safe. I will collect it all as we swap the clients around and all monies will be divvied up at the end of that business day."

"Oh, and just one other thing; anyone found stealing off our own will answer to Petra."

"Who do we come to if we have an issue, Hannah?"

"You come to me, only me, and my word is final!"

"Get to work, girls, we open in a couple of days from now," Petra shouted as I headed off to the kitchen for a cup of tea.

Heidi followed me. "Shouldn't you have told them about intelligence gathering Hannah?"

"No, Heidi, we are not going to use these girls for that. Is the bar set up?"

"Yes, everything's ready to go, - the only thing missing is our clients."

"Good, cuppa?"

"No thanks Hannah, I have to go and complete my reconnaissance of the surrounding area before we open."

"I thought we had got enough information about that Heidi?"

"No, there are some gaps which need filling. The British have asked me to gather intelligence of all manufacturing plants and buildings in and around the city, I will not be long."

Heidi had really taken to her role as intelligence officer; it was certainly her forte. The British had now supplied us another one of their gadgets; a radio aerial concealed in a washing line, which was much better for our situation.

The salon had now been open for a couple months, business was growing steadily, and we had been sending regular reports to Falcon and Viper, but we had still received no news about our first mission from them. I was starting to think it was never going to happen, but that was possibly a good thing as we didn't have enough girls to cover our absence.

The front door rolled open for the umpteenth time and in came clients on a steady basis. They are hoping to mask their worries and cloak their responsibilities with the taste for the delights that the building had to offer. Many chuckled aloud and laughed, sharing handshakes with signatory Nazi symbolisms, which I was finding harder and harder to swallow - even the sight of the uniform was bringing thoughts of hate to the front of my mind, while others simply raised their bottles to their lips and gave nods of approvals to the other clients using the brothel.

One thing was for sure - the girls were now building a solid, recurring client base. The weekends were the busiest, with some clients spending the whole weekend with the girls. It was great, but if it continued, we would need more girls and perhaps even a larger house.

The thick and pungent smell of tobacco, mixed with alcohol and other undecipherable items filled the air in murky cloud, while loud cheers broke through intermittently as Heidi worked her ass off to meet the needs of our drunken customers.

Nuremberg was a nice city, clean with hardly any signs of the war, unlike Berlin. The streets are full of uniformed soldiers and personnel and the population of the city seemed content. The only downside is, due to this city been Nazi rally headquarters, it is adorned with Nazi symbolism everywhere. There had been some bombing of the city in the past, but nothing like Berlin.

For now, it was business as usual at the brothel and the girls prepared for yet another busy day. It wasn't long before the clients started pouring in. Today was like most others apart from they seem to have a very high-ranking client just walked in with a friend. It was Hermann Goering, second only to Hitler himself. He was fatter than I had imagined; my parents had deep admiration for him due to his services in WWI, he was a great fighter pilot. They used to tell me stories about him all the time, he was one of my heroes throughout my early years.

Oh crap, Heidi thought to herself; she remembered him from the Kitty salon. He only liked certain things, so she went off to ensure that a couple of girls were okay with the request that was most certainly going to come.

"Can I offer you a drink?" Heidi asked.

"Champagne, two bottles," he replied.

"Herr Goering, I don't believe you have visited us before, it's a pleasure to serve you," I remarked as I took their coats and hats. He smiled and took a table with his friend. Serrano Suner was the brother-in-law of Francisco Franco, the Spanish head of state. Apparently, he and Goering spent a lot of time in salons when he visited Berlin, which was quite often as Suner bought art and other artefacts from Goering almost every few months.

Heidi told me that she remembered seeing them together a lot at Kitty's salon, they were as thick as thieves which was appropriate really, because it was a well-known fact that Goering had stolen most of the art he sold to Suner.

Heidi recalled that they always kicked off Suner's visit with a couple of days visiting a salon, then it was off to do their business. If they could look after them well and they became regular clients it would be a great move for us, so I selected a couple of exceptionally beautiful, totally stunning girls for Goering and one just as beautiful for Suner. Goering enjoyed lesbianism; it was his thing and if the girls could perform well, then it was certainly going to bring him back for more.

He always, paid very well and left a good tip. I asked Petra to instruct the girls not to try and steal anything from either of them. Furthermore, because of their stature it would not be a good move to insult or have two men as powerful as them as enemies.

After finishing their first bottle, they went to their rooms. No one saw them for well over six hours but the sounds coming from their rooms provided an insight into whether they were enjoying themselves or not, and it all sounded good so far. Goering ordered two more bottles of champagne and Heidi delivered them.

The issue now though was our other clients; we didn't have anyone to serve them.

"Petra, would you hit the streets and see if you can find a few more girls please, we are now well under-staffed."

"Okay, Hannah it's not going to be easy as we know from our last trawl of the streets, but I will do what I can. What are you going to do if someone comes in? We have no girls for them."

"I will have to be honest and tell them that we have a high-ranking party official in, and we are only able to offer minor services for the day, Petra."

"What the fuck? You and Heidi are going to...?"

"Yes, there are other ways to satisfy a man other than them climbing all over them, regardless of how much it actually repulses me. Besides, we have to be seen as an honest salon, Petra."

"I will be as quick as I can be, Hannah, but maybe we should have done this weeks ago."

"There is no need to state the obvious Petra, just go."

I now had to go and break the news to Heidi; this wasn't going to be an enjoyable conversation.

"I like what you have done with your hair, Heidi."

"Thank you, Hannah, it helps to hide my scars, gives me a little more confidence."

"Heidi, I have sent Petra out to find some more girls - we have no one to serve our regular clients at the moment and so it's up to us, you and me. We must do what we can to keep them."

"Are you saying what I think you're saying Hannah? You expect me to go back to laying on my back?"

"That is entirely up to you Heidi. We can't blow our cover now, we are supposed to be prostitutes, aren't we? There is more than one way to deal with a man's desires, we will have to do what we can until Petra returns."

"I thought we didn't have to do that anymore Hannah? It's bad enough having to run a brothel, now, we have to go through feeling like a piece of meat again, lose any kind of dignity and self-worth that we have now finally rebuilt."

"Heidi, I get you, being forced to do things we don't really want to do, getting hit and suffering a constant cycle of bruising from over-zealous clients really doesn't appeal to me either, but we are going to have to do whatever it takes at this time."

"Hannah, I realise that our world is now different to most others, not every road is straight. Sometimes they are curved, we have to deal with what we are given, I get it, I will do what whatever it takes. But I am not happy about it, you two mean *the world to me!*"

"Nor am I, Heidi, I feel sick to the stomach just talking about it, but it won't be for long."

The hours went by as did the flow of clients - some opted to return later rather than have myself or Heidi take care of them in a lesser manner than what they had come for. Finally, after six hours, Petra returned with two more girls who I quickly gave the speech to and got cleaned up and ready for work.

"Well done, Petra, but we need a couple more, I will go out over the next few days and see if I can find some."

"They were the only two I could find of the right age Hannah, there are some much older girls out there but to be honest, no good for us."

Later that day, Goering and Suner left and, just as Heidi had said, he paid very well and with a good tip.

"Danke, mein herr, I hope everything was to your satisfaction?" I asked him as I helped him on with his coat

"Yes, totally, I will visit here next time I am in Nuremberg," he replied, and they left.

The pressure was off for now, and so Petra had the two new girls introduce themselves to the others and started them working.

That evening Heidi, Petra and I decide to keep all the other girls out of the intelligence gathering, after all, all we had to do was listen to them gossip, and they are particularly good at that. We were now well established, and anyone of these girls could be an informant! We would require information to move forward. Petra asked me about the diamonds, and if I had forgotten about them.

"Not at all, Petra, but we need to be up to full working strength before we can make any kind of plans," I replied.

I asked Heidi to contact Falcon to see if there was any word regarding our first mission. It took two days for a reply which simply stated, *"continue establishing your cover, contact you soon."*

"I am beginning to think we made the wrong decision working for the British, Hannah," Heidi remarked.

To be honest, I was thinking the same thing; did they just want us to be their prostitutes informing them of German intelligence, or were we actually going to get to kill some of them? Stealing from them was only a minor hindrance; I wanted to make a much deeper impact than that.

Heidi and the girls were having a busy day, some of the girls had already seen three clients each and it was not even 18.00 yet, so a long night was ahead of them. I can't help thinking we might need more girls, more so if Goering or someone else came in that preferred two girls at a time. I would have to speak to Heidi and Petra later.

It was close to 03.00 before the last client left and we closed the door on yet another fruitful day. We were now making some really decent money on a daily basis.

All the girls seemed to be up early this morning, one after another they appeared in the kitchen, some looking a little worse for wear and one of the new girls wasn't at all well and needed to see a doctor. Everyone was busy getting prepared for the day ahead, one visited the doctor with what we thought was a sexually transmitted disease, whilst the others were cleaning, supply shopping from the black market whilst Heidi and Petra trawled the streets for new girls. Whilst I was going about my duties, I realised that I could use some of these girls as weapons. A sexually transmitted disease could put a soldier out of action for weeks - what a terrific way to destroy the physical condition of the Nazis! Infect as many as I could using some of my girls as carriers, was I really thinking this? More to the point, was I going to use it? Yes, I was. If she returned and stated she was infected, I would use any means possible. One thing in my favour was the fact that these soldiers use many different brothels so they would not know where they got infected!

As part of my late schooling, we had had a class on this very subject. I remembered two very important facts from that class: one, prevention, always use a condom, and two, treatment, although the Nazis are so far involved in promoting the cleansing of our country through the final solution, they have overlooked this particular problem. Treatment for such diseases was lengthy and it did have some life-long side effects as we were informed in our class; skin infections, bones, internal organs, nerves and cardio systems were all irreversibly damaged by these diseases, even after treatment by mercury pills or creams. Had I just stumbled upon a method that will have a lasting effect on the Nazis? Something that is self-inflicting through their own arrogance? Later that day the girl returned, and she had indeed contracted syphilis.

"Follow me into the kitchen," I asked her.

"Here is the issue, if you don't work then you can't pay the house, if you're not paying your way then you're out on the streets."

"But Hannah, if I continue working then I might infect others?" she replied.

"I don't care, look, for one month, I will reduce your percentage payable to the house to 25% if you keep working, encourage everyone not to use a condom and share the disease with as many as you can, but you're to tell no one about this, and I mean NO ONE!"

"What happens after the month?"

"You will get yourself treated and whilst that is happening, the money you have saved over the month will help you pay your way here during your treatment."

She understood her options were limited. "I have nowhere else to go, so I have no choice."

"I guess you don't, and remember to tell no one of this, or you're out."

"No, Madam Hannah."

At least I didn't have to ask permission from the British about this. After all, sexually transmitted diseases were common in brothels.

"Petra, I need to speak with you."

"Yes, Hannah?"

She took me aside. "That girl who attended the doctor has syphilis; she will continue to work at a reduced rate for one month."

"Are you fucking serious? That will infect our clients!" she exclaimed.

"I know, that is the plan, this is between us only, you have to know as you're in charge of the girls. Make sure she only services new clients and make it known to them that she likes it without a condom."

"You want me to encourage this?"

"That's the idea yes, Petra, I want her to infect as many soldiers as she can."

"Oh, that's clever Hannah. Cold hearted, but clever. But what of the girl?"

"She will be looked after once she starts treatment."

"Now, did you find anymore girls today?"

"Possibly, we will have to see who turns up," Petra continued, "We have now approached most of them on the streets, we are running out of possibilities Hannah."

"We will just have to work with what we have, Petra."

"No problem, it's going to start getting busy around here. When do you think we will hear from the British about our first mission?"

"I really don't know, that's why I decided to use that infected girl, at least we are doing something now, Petra."

"I am with you; it doesn't matter how we get them as long as we do."

The brothel continued to grow. We had plenty of regulars now, and even top industrialists from other countries were using us. We were also gathering some remarkably interesting information. It was quite shocking to some of us what the Nazis were taking or had taken from people that fell into certain categories: Jews, Gypsies, the disabled and so on. They took everything worth any value, most of which went directly to help their war efforts, but there was so much of it that most of the high-ranking officers were getting rich from. Petra, Heidi and I discussed this from time to time and decided it might be a promising idea to start using some of this information to further line our own pockets. Steal from those that steal! It could only be a win-win situation. After all, they couldn't tell anyone if they were robbed. We were already stealing a little extra cash from just about every client, so the next natural step was to steal more. So, we looked at different methods we could use to this end.

One new great skill we had all learnt about was the art of misdirection, which could come in especially useful for just those types of situations that required keeping people busy to mask what was really going on. Petra started to follow a select few of our client's home at the end of the evening so we could begin to gather personal information on them for future reference.

The following week I finally received a message from Falcon.

"Meet tomorrow at the café."

Was this it, our first mission? The day couldn't go fast enough for me, I was both excited and nervous at the same time.

The time had come, so I left for the meeting. I arrived a few minutes early to ensure a table far enough away from listening ears, although the café wasn't really that busy anyway, but I found a quiet corner where I had an unobstructed view of the whole place. To my surprise, it was actually Viper that arrived at the meeting, I asked why Falcon hadn't come himself.

"He had to return to London," Viper replied. "He will return in a couple of days."

Viper looked up as a waiter approached. "Two teas, please."

"I am only allowed to tell you this much at this time Hannah – we have managed to piece together information from you and from the Italian resistance that there is to be a party for high-ranking officers to celebrate their recent endeavours in the area."

"Italy? When is this party to take place?" I asked.

"We are still waiting for confirmation of the date, but we think this coming January, so in eight weeks' time or so."

"Our target?"

"Again, still waiting on confirmation, but we do have information that a transport lieutenant will be in attendance and he will be carrying some important documents," Viper continued. "We will contact you again as soon as we have all the information verified."

"Right, can you provide all the intelligence about the area so we can at least start familiarising ourselves with that?"

"Everything we have so far is in this newspaper. Tensions are high in Italy so be careful, there are many that hate Germany and just as many that hate Mussolini for joining Hitler."

Viper finished her tea and left me to finish mine. Finally, we were getting to use some of our newfound skills. This was it – our first mission.

I returned to the salon and brought Heidi and Petra up to speed, asking Heidi to prepare a briefing of the general area twenty miles south of Rome, Italy. Escape routes were our main concern at this point from the information in the paper provided by Viper. Petra was just as excited as I was; the excitement was permeated by a large dose of anxiety, but we had to concentrate on our mission; soon we would get to take out some more Nazis.

The British never rushed anything, and it took another ten days before we received the full details of the mission. I noticed in the paper that Berlin was now being bombed day and night; the Americans were bombing during the day whilst the British continued night-time bombing. I was so pleased we decided not to return to Berlin; we might not have survived it a second time.

The mission brief was as follows: we would pose as hired female entertainment at a party for high-ranking officers based in Italy. The party would be full of local prostitutes, so we would fit in perfectly. It would take place in Frascati village, twenty miles south of Rome, Saturday 9th January 1943, at the Villa Aldobrandini.

Our target was a transport lieutenant called Ernst Heinrich. He would be carrying top secret Axis movement intelligence and would be using the villa as an over-night stop on his way to Berlin.

He usually travelled with one guard, who rarely left his sight.

Our objective – one of the girls would seduce Heinrich at the party and allow him to take her up to his room. His guard would not follow him into his room, as this was the only place he was ever alone. This girl would be Petra. I would work on the guard and entice him into another room, where I would kill him.

All parties had to be killed silently, all documentation had to be secured, and we would travel to and from Italy by train, with a driver by the Italian resistance to get us to and from the villa. He would also supply us with Italian-style dresses for the party.

This gave us six weeks to prepare and I could already feel the anxiety building up inside me – or was it excitement? To be honest, I wasn't really sure.

Chapter Eight

Heidi

"Hannah, do you recall me telling you that the British wanted intelligence on manufacturing plants in the area?"

"Yes, Heidi."

"Well, I have just found out why, they are going to start bombing Nuremberg like they are bombing Berlin, day and night."

"That's why they wanted the information Hannah, they don't care that we are here, we are expendable to them," Heidi continued.

"But the Allies miss their targets by miles? The British are the worst, I can't live through that again, the fear of being buried alive is unbelievable, Hannah!"

Hannah

Suddenly I found myself in some sort of a trance. I could feel my hand moving over my clothes where my body was scarred by burns from Berlin, the discomfort and pain that I suffered for weeks came flooding back. These thoughts happened on many occasions to be honest. Sometimes, when I washed or bathed, the strange texture of my skin when I ran my hands over my scars made me feel repulsed. The next thing I remembered was seeing Heidi laid on the floor; she must have fainted.

"Heidi, Heidi, are you alright?" I asked desperately.

"Give me a moment, Hannah. I will be okay, I just..."

"You are shaking all over Heidi, and you look as white as a sheet."

It seemed that just the thought of being entombed in darkness again was enough to affect every part of her senses, Heidi had lost any control she had of her body, she was gripped and crippled with fear.

"Sorry Hannah, I had sudden flash backs, it was like I was back in Berlin all over again," Heidi stated as she ran her fingers over her face, checking her hands for blood.

"You're okay Heidi, look, there's no blood, you're here with me in the kitchen," I assured her.

"When are they going to start the bombing, Heidi?" I asked.

"Not sure Hannah, but after seeing how it has affected me, I started looking at ways we could possibly help the Allies keep their bombing runs on target!"

"And what have you come up with Heidi?"

"Help me up, Hannah, and I will show you what I have."

"They miss most targets at night, right, so if they are to work off the list that I complied and start using incendiary devices running off long timed fuses, to give us enough time to get away and not get caught, these set the targets alight which would act as a beacon for the bombers."

"Sounds good to me, but how will they know this, Heidi?"

"I have sent a clear coded message and so hopefully it should filter down to the British bomber command within a day or so, requesting they follow my list working from the top down and three targets per night, also to time their bombing raid for 3am every night."

"Okay Heidi, I will collect the incendiaries and hide them so we are ready, but surely we will need some help with this?"

"We have no help. If you don't want the whole city bombed, then this is the quickest way to help prevent that."

"I hope it works Heidi, you remain here, Petra and I will go and set the beacons of flames for the bombers tonight."

It's hard enough bombing a target during the day, constantly adjusting for wind, height and speed, but at night, it's ten times harder. This is why Berlin was now such a tangle mass of rubble and ruins - they just couldn't see where they were dropping their bombs. This plan of Heidi's might just tip the balance - not just for their aim but for our survival too.

That evening, Petra and I went off to set the first three factories ablaze but as we travelled to the area, I noticed that there was low laying cloud and so maybe it was a futile move as they normally bomb from high altitude. We also didn't know for sure that the message Heidi had sent had got through yet, but we had to try anyway.

"Hannah, I am so nervous."

"Yes, me too, Petra..."

"Do you think it ever goes away? I mean the more we do, will we feel these emotions less?"

"Probably not, but the good thing is that we are outside, so if we need to throw up we can."

Following the map drawn by Heidi so that we missed most of the areas with high concentrations of soldiers we made our way to the first target, a munitions factory. Heidi had selected an area where they stored the gun powder, Petra cut a hole in the fence...

"Wait, dogs - they have dog patrols, Petra."

"Does it say anything about dogs on the map, Hannah?"

"No, it could be that they have only just introduced them, Heidi wouldn't leave something like that out."

"We will have to miss this one out for now Hannah, we have no way to deal with dogs, besides, I don't like dogs."

"Agreed, we will find another way in at a later date."

We made our way across a small river to the next target, which was a textile factory. I didn't understand why this was on the target list though, I would ask Heidi when we return.

There was no fence or dogs at this factory, and we placed the incendiary timed bombs where Heidi had indicated for maximum impact. Even if the planes missed their target this factory would be out of action for some time.

On to our third target (the railway station that transported goods in and out of the city) which was only a few hundred metres away. Most of the Nuremberg industry was in the southern part of the city, so hopefully once they saw the other two burning buildings, they would concentrate their bombing in that area. We had done all we could on the ground. Now it was a waiting game.

We arrived back at the salon by 02.15. The skies began to hum, a sound I instantly recognised; the Allied planes were coming, and they were early. I spent all night stood mostly in the street with Heidi; the fear of being buried again was so strong she couldn't fight it, listening in fear as the planes flew overhead and that terrifying whistling sound as the bombs dropped through the air, watching as the night sky turned an orange colour from the fires.

As the hours passed, I watched and witnessed our efforts failing! I could see that from the direction of the flames the old town had been hit several times. The old town was mostly constructed from timber and so it would not be standing for long as the flames would consume building after building as they were built so close to each other.

By daybreak I was sat on the front steps of the salon, I knew that it would only be a matter of time before Nuremberg was going to become another Berlin, a city laid to death and ruins. Petra came looking for me as I wasn't sat in my normal place in the kitchen that morning.

"Hannah, are you okay? Your bed hasn't been slept in, have you been out here all night?"

"Yes, I couldn't come in. I stayed with Heidi."

"The bombs were falling miles away, to the south, nowhere near us here Hannah."

"Heidi, we failed, I saw the old town had been hit and if you look you can see it's still burning."

"At least we tried, Petra, that's more than most have done. Come, we have to prepare for the day ahead."

We headed into the kitchen where we prepared some bread and fruit for breakfast.

"It was a complete failure, Petra," I said as I sat down at the table and placed my head down onto my arms.

"Yes, I was watching out the window, Hannah."

The next few hours seemed to go by in a blur. Around 18.00 Heidi came looking for me with news from Falcon, which simply stated:

"You will have to take your chances like everyone else."

"I told you, Hannah - to the British we are expendable. It is war and they will not stop bombing just because we are here."

"I can't see you go through that again Heidi, it's time to take care of ourselves. We have five weeks until we have to be in Italy, yes?" Heidi nodded, and I continued, "Right, let's take another look at that information on the courier, and Heidi, you find us somewhere to relocate."

While Heidi compiled the information I requested, I spoke with Petra about leaving Nuremberg with a special gift—well some of the Nazis living there, that is.

"What do you have in mind Hannah?"

"We have a good supply of the poison, right? So, I think we should inject it into all the booze we have on the premises the night before we decide to leave."

"What about the other girls, they also drink that booze, Hannah!"

"Victims of circumstance, Petra."

"Now that is fucking cold, callous even," said Petra.

"I need to know if this stuff works before we take on the diamond courier. Besides, we are leaving this city, the Allies are dropping bombs and so pretty soon this place will be in total ruins. Everyone will be trying to just survive! they won't care why or how any Nazis and prostitutes have died."

"There are certainly plenty of people leaving Nuremberg to escape the bombing, which will provide us with plenty of cover. I agree, we should test it out first."

It took Heidi several days to find us a secluded farmhouse thirty kilometres away from Nuremberg to the south. We took it in turns to travel down there to prepare the place, taking food, our radio, some clothing and other small items that we needed.

Heidi sent a communication to Falcon informing him we were relocating to the south out of the way of the bombings and would be out of contact for several days until we were settled.

The next evening, I took a syringe and injected the poison into all the alcohol in the salon. I sent Heidi down to the farmhouse to prepare the plan for the courier, then Petra and I left and opened the salon for the business of the day.

It was a shame to leave the brothel, but we really had no choice. The fear I saw in Heidi's eyes was real, she really was terrified of being bombed again. It was far too deep, and we could no longer stay here.

Petra and I had a busy day. Once the clients and girls started drinking, they started dropping like flies. The bodies started piling up in every room, so periodically we locked the doors and moved them into one room. We wanted to stay open as long as we could on our last day - as long as the alcohol didn't run out, there was no point in wasting good poison!

As the girls had all died, Petra and I would now lead the clients into different rooms, telling them that a girl would be with them shortly. Of course, we left them with a bottle to drink while they waited.

"This stuff is fast acting, Hannah. I am knackered trying to keep up. I need help with one in this room, he is a little heavy."

"Yes, it certainly is, almost instant acting, Petra."

We didn't have to move the heavy guy as we had run out of alcohol. It was time to close and lock the doors for good. We stayed until darkness fell and we heard the bombers doing their nightly run. After dousing the place with fuel and setting it alight, we left for the last time. The flames wouldn't be an issue as people would think the brothel was hit by a bomb, covering our tracks nicely.

Chapter Nine

"Petra? How do you feel about visiting a few cafés with me and picking up as many high-ranking officers as we can?"

"For what reason, Hannah?"

"Only one reason, Petra - kill as many Nazis as we can before we leave Nuremberg for good."

"That will surely draw attention to us?"

"We can disguise ourselves in different ways. If we don't use the same cafes every night, we can surely get a good few of them. Look, we pick them up on the promise of sex, as soon as they have us alone, we strike. According to Falcon it only takes one little prick or scratch from the ring."

"I am usually with you Hannah, but this is fucking madness, it will draw far too much attention, and what about the British? What if they find out what we are doing?"

"Petra, the British only care about their own missions, and besides, isn't defeating the Nazis the Allies' main objective anyway? In my mind, we are helping them with that, soldiers are dying everywhere, the British don't have time or the resources to check every dead German soldier."

We decided that we would travel separately south, once Petra had seen my plan in action and of course that it worked, calling at as many cafés and bars and killing as many high-ranking officers as we could along the route as we left the city.

I was getting a taste for this now, the first few I killed I felt sick to my stomach. Now it was like I had ice water in my veins; I felt nothing. All I cared about was ridding the world of as many of these narrow minded, heartless people as possible. The one thing I didn't realise was by doing this I had become the very thing I now hated the most in my world. The difference was, I was a woman, and so at least they went out with a nice last thought, unlike the terrified people in those horrible camps scattered around the country.

Petra and I continued heading south.

I sat in a small café with Petra watching from a distance. It wasn't long before I attracted the attentions of an SS officer.

"Good evening, fraulein," he said as he approached.

I smiled as he sat at my table and returned the greeting.

"May I buy you a drink?"

"Thank you, sir. Schnapps, please."

The small talk continued for about twenty minutes or so - he made it obvious what he wanted. Just like all German officers; they took what they wanted, when they wanted it and as an Aryan female I was supposed to conform to his desires.

I am staying just around the corner. Come, let's have a drink there?" He held his hand out to help me from my chair.

He wasn't joking, it only took a couple of minutes to reach his residence. It was a simple single room which was typical of an officer of his lower-rank status. He took my coat and I went over to stand by the fireplace as he poured me a drink.

"Now isn't this much nicer, just the two of us. Tell me, what is your name?"

"Hannah." I didn't have to lie as he was going to be dead very soon.

He continued asking me questions about my age, where I lived, all the normal small talk that generally builds up to the inevitable touching and kissing. He started by stroking my arm, moving in even closer. He took my glass and placed it on the mantle, before putting his hand on the small of my back and pulling me in close. I instinctively put my hands over his shoulders as he moved in closer. As I popped the top of the ring, he moved in and started kissing me. With one simple quick stab to the side of his neck, his passion instantly turned to stone. This poison was extremely fast acting, he now stood in front of me, not able to speak or move, like a statue. It was almost instantaneous; all I could hear from him was his attempt to draw breath. I watch as the life slowly withdrew from his eyes, although not painlessly I don't think.

This poison was strong, we had to be incredibly careful with it. I searched him for anything of value and left the room to meet up with Petra.

"All good?" she asked, relieved to see me.

I simply said nothing, just showed her what I had taken from him and that I had no marks on me whatsoever. "This is easy pickings, Petra."

"What do you think about just before you kill someone, Hannah?"

"Um, well. It's like I have a silent movie running through my head, Petra, images of everyone that has being taken from, my parents, my friends, Regina, my body and all the pain and suffering they have put me through. Once that runs a couple of times in my mind, my reaction is almost automatic! What about you?"

"Yes, somewhat the same, it is certainly getting easier and easier."

"Ok, let's keep going."

"Easy pickings this might be, Hannah, but you're forgetting one thing - we are running out of room for all this stuff. If we are going to keep killing all the way to Heidi, then we are going to need a suitcase to carry all the loot."

"What are you saying, Petra? We should stop?"

"Look, this fucking killing spree you have us on is great, but our pockets are full, so are we just going to kill for the hell of it or steal a suitcase and at least have a reason to kill?"

"Whatever helps you sleep at night, Petra. As for me, I am not doing this for some kind of meaningless material things, I am doing this for the great good of our country and if I make a few marks along the way then that's a bonus."

"One thing is for sure Hannah - once you commit to something you certainly give it your all."

We continued to head in a southerly direction and split up. It was safer to travel alone, calling at bars and cafés as we travelled. It actually turned into somewhat of a game, keeping a tally as we went. As we had no intention to return, we hadn't bothered too much with disguises and anyway, we looked just like any ordinary German women would.

It felt good to me, to be finally giving some much-needed attention to the only thing that fuelled my existence - revenge, payback for all they had taken from me, my family, my country and my dignity.

I arrived at the farmhouse and Heidi was already set up, having sent a coded message to Falcon giving our current position and status.

Although we were staying in a farmhouse, there were no farm animals at all; it had belonged to a Jewish family and so the Nazis took all the stock for their own consumption.

That night was calm and quiet. The only sounds I could hear came from the creatures of the night, owls hooting and the odd sound of rodents shuffling about searching for food. Again, I was taken back to my family home in peaceful times, but also remembered our days in the hill-top forest cabin when we first met Falcon and Viper.

The next day Heidi took us through her plan for the diamond courier, which to be honest was to say the least, somewhat ambiguous. This wasn't her fault though as we really didn't have enough information for a clear plan.

We knew he travelled the first weekend of every month; we knew his route and what he looked like.

I suggested to Heidi that we travel to Rome. We had money, and to be honest, plenty of it, from the brothel, so we had no problem getting down there and finding a hotel to stay in. At least then we could have a good look around.

I asked Heidi to contact Falcon for a meet-up, as we needed travel documents and he could provide them, if he agreed to us travelling to Rome on a reconnaissance mission in readiness for our actual mission next year. It soon became apparent that our rather hasty move out of Nuremberg hadn't gone down well with Falcon. I was woken early by the sound of people arguing, it was 05.20 and Falcon had arrived at the farmhouse in a bad mood. I quickly threw a coat on and entered the kitchen where Falcon and Heidi were having a shouting match.

"Who gave you permission to leave the brothel?" he shouted at Heidi.

"It wasn't..." Heidi started to reply but I cut in.

"It was me! I couldn't stand by anymore and watch the emotional strain on Heidi, the sounds of the planes and bombs dropping turned her into a quivering wreck, I had to get her out of there."

"Oh, and you didn't think to contact us first?"

"It was my decision, mine alone. If you have an issue with it then take it out on me, they were following my orders."

At this point Petra had woken up and entered the kitchen. "What the fuck is going on?" she asked.

"He isn't happy we left Nuremberg without clearing it with them first, Petra," I explained.

"Who gives a shit what he thinks," stated Petra as she poured a cup of coffee.

I turned back to Falcon and presented our case. "Your last message said that we would have to take our chances like the rest of the population of Nuremberg. Well, I wasn't going to be buried alive again, not again, and I certainly wasn't going to let Heidi go through that nightmare again. You told me once that we have to be ready to adjust and be prepared for any situation, didn't you?"

"Yes..."

I cut him off before he could say more. "Then as far as I can tell, we are alive, unhurt and out of danger, so how is that not being prepared and adjusting to the situation? We have all witnessed first-hand how badly the British aim with your bombs, and Petra and I were not going to allow Heidi to go through that again."

"I understand why you moved but you should have waited for us to find you a safe place. This farmhouse, whose is it and how did you find it?"

"I contacted the local police and asked them for information on unoccupied Jewish homes in the countryside for rent, I told them that as prostitutes from Nuremberg we needed a place for us as a retreat, for a break. He checked our papers, it all matches up, we are clear for the moment," replied Heidi.

"Okay, well as it happens the brothel - along with most of the city - is now in ruins."

He didn't mention anything about any bodies being found which had died from unforeseen issues, so I guess we got away with that, possibly as a direct result of the bombings masking the string of assassinations.

"We need to get you all to a safer place, this is okay for a few days but you're going to have to move," said Falcon.

"I have a plan for that Falcon, we think it would be a good idea if we went down to Rome, so we can do a full recon of the area and prepare correctly for the mission ahead, what do you think?" stated Heidi.

"Given the current situation, I think it's a good move, it will provide us with time to relocate you on a more permanent basis."

"We will need travel documents and any resistance contacts you have in the area," I requested.

"Right then, Hannah. I will return in a few days. In the meantime, destroy everything you don't need to take with you, including the radio. Bury it all."

"We will be ready and waiting."

Falcon left and it seemed to me that he was satisfied with my explanation for going to Rome. I still felt the less he knew about the diamonds, the better. We spent the morning destroying the equipment we didn't need, we sorted out clothing that wasn't required and buried it along with all the jewellery Petra and I had stolen from the Germans we had killed on our way out of Nuremberg.

That afternoon we had a surprise visit from the local police. Something we had not considered at all was their instinctive nature to be nosy as well as a man's natural desire to conquer as many beautiful women as he could.

"Good afternoon, ladies," he shouted as he closed the door to his vehicle.

Petra let out a false cough to get my attention, looking down at her ring and giving a little nod. I gave a slight nod of disapproval, hoping she had received the message. The last thing we needed now is another dead body, more so one that was a well-known local police officer. We would need to approach this situation with far more tact.

"Good afternoon," I replied. "How may we help you?"

"I thought I would see how you are settling in; do you have everything you need?"

"Yes, thank you, it's very peaceful here, just what we need at the moment."

"Here, I have a bottle of wine for you as a gift."

"Danke, mein herr. Please take a glass with us." I offered.

It was quite clear to me that he had not come here for a glass of wine. Luckily, Petra was on the ball too.

"Mein herr, let me take care of you. Come, please come inside." Taking his arm, she led him inside.

"That was close, if he had been a few minutes earlier he would have seen us burying our stuff, Hannah," said Heidi.

"Yes, it's also lucky that Petra was here, otherwise it would have had to be you who satisfied his only real reason for coming here."

"We only have a few days before Falcon returns with the travel documents, it's a small price to pay Hannah. Anyway, Petra likes men."

After an hour or so the officer left, but we all knew we would be seeing him again. We spent the rest of the day just lazing around and recharging, going over and over the information we had on the courier until it was imprinted on our minds. Then we burned the paperwork.

After a couple of days Falcon returned with our travel documents. It was quite astounding to me just how much the British knew about the Nazis and their infostructure; the documents they reproduced were outstanding.

"Hannah, I suggest you stay in Italy until the mission in three weeks' time, it will be safer for you there," said Falcon as he handed them over to me.

"What is our exit plan?" I asked.

"You can use what means you think, but you will need to get to Switzerland, I have included your border paperwork dated for the 11th January and the contact details of one of our agents there. That's two days after the mission, so don't hang about."

Falcon left and we prepared to get going; we had only three weeks to get the diamonds and prepare for the British mission.

Chapter Ten

It was Friday December 18th and the station was packed with soldiers and family members travelling to see their families for Christmas. To help us blend in, we carried small wrapped gifts that we had purchased, supposedly for our own families.

The train pulled into the concourse and it took several minutes for the passengers to disembark the train. Passengers stood well back on the platform, allowing what seemed like a never-ending stream of people to exit the platform. It was like watching a stream of ants, all heading in the same direction with one single objective: find the exit.

The train pulled out on time and now we had just over twenty-four hours until we reached Rome. With this train being an overnight train, we had our own cabin; it was small but cosy, with four single beds, one over the other. Each carriage had its own bathroom.

This time provided plenty of opportunity for contemplation, going over the mission in our heads and discussing quietly any potential issues again and again. I asked Heidi if she was okay as she had gone a little too quiet.

"Yes, I just didn't think I was going to have a life like this, Hannah. It's really quite exciting, isn't it?"

"I suppose so, Heidi."

"I think that joining the British was a clever idea Hannah, it means we get to visit some wonderful places that otherwise we might never have had the chance to visit."

"Yes, I have to agree Heidi, but we must also remember why we are doing this. Our mission is the important thing here," Petra chipped in.

"Maybe so, Petra, but that doesn't mean we have to miss out and not take any notice of the scenery," stated Heidi

"No, but let's not let it distract us though; we must stay focused," replied Petra.

"It's not good what the Germans are doing when they take control of a country, they take everything they want. I can't help but wonder how much they have taken over the past year or so, all in the name of contributing to the war and the Fuhrer," Heidi replied.

"Hopefully we are going to start balancing the scales a little, and yes, we get something out of it, but we are also helping to prevent funds entering their pockets. It is only a drop in the ocean, but everything we do no matter how little is for a compelling cause."

"Ours!" Petra commented.

"Let's go and find the restaurant car." I was starting to feel hungry.

Lunch time had soon arrived and so we headed off to the restaurant car. We were passing through Austria now; the scenery was quite amazing, the snow-covered Alps in the distance with the valleys only giving away that they had residences by the smoking chimneys sporadically dotted around. None of us had seen so much snow - it was like a different world without any signs of the war whatsoever anywhere. This trip was by far the longest one we had taken, and would be the first time any of us have visited another country. Almost every country Hitler and his Nazi party had invaded or annexed showed some signs of the war, but not Austria. Maybe it was because it was Hitler's home country, or maybe there was simply nothing there of interest to the Allies. Maybe I hadn't seen enough of the country to comment, but what I had seen so far was beautiful and war free.

Lunch arrived and consisted of pea soup and then some stew, this was fast becoming part of our daily diet. The Nazis had implemented these types of meals some time ago. They consisted of three main things - they had to be cheap, sanctioned by the Nazis and came in one pot. There really wasn't a lot to choose from. During our lunch we chatted about anything but the war. Hair, makeup, anything but the war. After lunch we retired back to our cabin, and Petra decided to get some rest. Heidi and I talked some more for a while, she had done some further research on why Hitler had invaded North Africa and she informed me:

"Hitler took North Africa for strategic reasons as it provides a staging point for the Mediterranean Sea, and of course for its natural resources, one of which is diamonds."

"Heidi." Admiringly. "You are a wealth of information. Intelligence truly is your thing, isn't it?"

"If there is one thing, I have come to realise Hannah, knowledge is everything. The more we know, the better off we will be. Did you know that a one carat diamond, depending on clarity and colour, can be worth as much as 800RM, which is almost half a year's skilled worker's salary in Germany?"

"That's a lot, Heidi."

"I have been thinking over the past couple of days, maybe it's a better idea if you two go to Ostia to wait for the courier. You will be able to check on the boat's arrival time and it's a much smaller station, so it will be easier to find our target."

"Let's look at what you have, Heidi."

"As you can see from the map, the station at Ostia is a one-track station. In fact, the only route it takes is direct to Rome, so the courier would certainly be easier to spot and then follow." Heidi continued, "The station building itself is small and again is linked to the seaport. There is also a small bus station which is situated adjacent to the train station, so you could watch both stations at the same time."

"You might be right Heidi. Okay, Petra and I will go and deal with that whilst you do your thing."

"I am going to try and get some sleep Hannah."

"Sleep well, Heidi."

By the time morning arrived, we were travelling well through Italy and the sun was shining. Within a few hours we would be coming into Rome.

The grinding sound from the train's wheels finally came to a halt and alerted the passengers to the journey's end, who began making their preparations to leave. We headed for the station exit and found a café to sit in whilst Petra went off to find a hotel and Heidi checked the train listings for the train from Ostia.

"Trains from the port of Ostia where the boat from Africa comes in arrive every hour, Hannah, so we will have to take it in turns to sit in the station to watch for him."

"Do you know what time the boat should arrive at Ostia Heidi? We can't sit around the train station all day every day, it will draw too much attention."

"Not yet Hannah, I will make some enquires."

"We have a few days, so no problem. It's Christmas time and we are in a foreign country, so let's just relax and take in our surroundings."

Petra arrived back, and she had found us a hotel just around the corner, so we finished our coffee and headed off. After checking in, we decided to go for a walk around Rome and visit some of the sights it had to offer, like the Colosseum and Vatican City.

Although it was wintertime, we were told it very rarely snows in Rome and anyway, the temperature was way too high, even in December. The streets were filled with echoing sounds of Christmas songs "Bianco Natale" (White Christmas) and "Astro del ceil" (Silent Night) performed by all manner of people, singing everywhere from cafes to churches. For a few short days everyone was immersed in the spirit of the festive season. In our hotel room we drank wine and exchanged the gifts that we had bought as part of our travel cover.

It was the 27th and our Italian contact had arrived. He wanted to take us down to the village where the villa was situated so we could do a full recon of the area.

"Hannah, I think it is best if I go alone," Heidi said.

"Why?" I wondered, not certain about splitting up.

"I can pose with the Italian as his wife, just out for a little sightseeing trip. It's the perfect cover."

"Okay, I agree, but nothing else, okay? Just recon, and not too close."

Petra and I packed a small bag for a couple of days, headed off to the station and left Heidi to do what she does best. The trains to Ostia left every hour or so, and so we didn't have a long wait.

Upon reflection, this was a particularly clever idea of Heidi's. There were so many variables regarding this situation; it was better to close them down if we could, one of them being the weather. If the boat hit harsh weather, it would be delayed.

One thing we were sure of was the trains for Berlin from Rome; one on Saturday 2nd and one on Sunday 3rd January, both at 09.00. So, we could have simply waited for both trains for Berlin, but if we did then we might have missed an opportunity to get the diamonds.

We arrived in Ostia and found a hotel, then it was down to the docks to gather as much information as possible about the boat from Africa. On-route, we walked past a small café with a strong aroma of coffee. Italian coffee could be quite strong, but I found it very pleasing.

"We don't have much time to waste on drinking coffee, Hannah, after all we don't want to miss the boat from Africa, do we?" asked Petra as the waitress placed our coffee on the table.

"You haven't missed it, ladies," stated the waitress. "It will be arriving at 10.00 in the morning."

"That just saved us a trip to the docks, Hannah."

"Maybe, Petra - you must be more careful though."

"Oh, you're just paranoid. Better to ask at a café than at the docks. Two young ladies like us asking about boat arrivals; nobody down there would forget that."

"You might be right, Petra."

We spent the rest of the day resting and sampling Italian pasta and wine. The next morning, we both took up our positions. There were only two directions the courier could take to the train station and we had them covered.

It was 10.25 and a steady stream of people started heading towards the train station. I spotted a man, wearing a trench coat, carrying a small suitcase and walking with a limp. I followed him into the station and sure enough he headed straight for the Rome platform. Within minutes of my arrival Petra turned up.

"I have him, Hannah! Look, there at the newspaper stand."

"What? No, I have him, Petra, he is sat on the bench on the platform waiting for the train."

"There are two of them, Hannah!"

"One must be a decoy, Petra."

"Yes, but which one? How can we tell them apart?"

"The Nazis are not stupid, very clever of them to use a decoy. So, they both have a false left leg, both men are dressed differently but about the same in most other ways. They would only entrust a high-ranking Gestapo man with this type of work Petra, so get a closer look at your man."

"Meet you on the train, Hannah."

The Gestapo were always very well groomed and proud of their appearance, so we were looking for anything out of place on either man. It was indoctrinated into them from the beginning of their training and the standards were high. We could always tell them apart from others at the brothel, but then the Nazis trained us for that.

The men stayed well away from each other, boarding the train at different ends and never looking at each other at all. I got myself in a position so I could get very close to the one I was following. I purposely bumped into him; he didn't speak but merely glared at me. I now had all the information I wanted about his appearance, the style and type of clothes he wore, and his approximate sizes, so I headed off to find Petra. We met up in the restaurant car. Petra had ordered some coffee.

"What did you find out Petra?"

"He is very well groomed, nothing out of place, he is wearing a nice suit, not German but genuinely nice clothes all the same, shoes polished and tied neatly. And, of course, he is wearing a 'death head ring'."

"I don't think my man is the courier. He needs a shave and a wash, and his clothing is old and smells musty. No way he is Gestapo, so we will go with yours Petra, yes?"

"Alright, Hannah, best choice. What is the plan?"

"This train is far too crowded; we will have to follow him and wait for our chance."

It took a couple of hours before we reached Rome, and we also knew that the courier would have to stay overnight as he had already missed today's train to Berlin. We followed him out of the station and couldn't believe our luck, he went straight into the same hotel we were staying in and got a room.

"Petra, you stay on watch and I will go drop our bag in our room, I will be back in a couple of hours to relieve you."

I freshened up and return to Petra after a couple of hours. There wasn't any sign of Heidi and so I guessed she was out doing her thing.

"Anything happening Petra?"

"No, he hasn't moved out of there."

"Go get yourself sorted; I have this for now. Oh, and there's no sign of Heidi, so keep an eye open for her."

"Will do. I'll be back in a couple of hours or so."

Petra had only been gone several minutes when a very nicely dressed young man approached the courier's door. He knocked, the door swung open and I couldn't believe what I saw next. Things just got even more complicated.

I hurried off to find Petra and bring her up to speed, although I still couldn't believe what I had seen myself. As I entered our room Petra was washing. She could tell something wasn't right by the look on my face.

"Hannah, what is wrong, is he on the move?"

I shook my head in a small motion from side to side, rolled my eyes and placed a single finger on my lips.

"What is it? Hannah, what the fucking hell has happened?"

"You're not going to believe this, Petra," I said as I sat on the bed, still shaking my head.

"Believe what?"

"This just got much harder, almost impossible in fact."

"Why, Hannah? Tell me, what is it?"

"The courier, you can forget any idea of seducing him to get close to him."

"Really? Why?"

"He's a homosexual! Completely disgusting and he should be shot, but he is into men."

"Are you sure? What did you see?"

"He has a young man in his room right now."

"That doesn't mean he is one, Hannah."

"Maybe not, but the fact that they had a full-on kiss as he closed the door does - I almost threw up!"

"Holy shit! Well, each to their own, I don't judge people's sexual preferences Hannah, but what the hell are we going to do now?"

"I am going to need a moment, Petra; I need to process this."

"This was supposed to be easy, Hannah, seduce him, kill him, steal the diamonds!"

"He certainly isn't going to be interested in anything any of us have to offer, is he? But one thing is for sure, he will soon become part of the final solution program, dead!"

At this point Heidi returned. She had had much better luck than we did. She was full of smiles and excitement. That was, until I told her about our day. As we didn't have long before the courier left for Berlin, we concentrated on finding a way around the seduction issue. We needed to get him alone and out of the public eye. Heidi sat, quietly scribbling on a piece of paper for about thirty minutes. I paced around the room and Petra continued with getting cleaned up. Suddenly, Heidi jumped to her feet.

"I have it!"

"Have what, Heidi?" I asked.

"We get a man's suit and one of us dresses up as a man. He likes young men, one of us could pass as a young man, right?"

"And what do you suggest we do about these, Heidi?" I said, indicating my breasts. "We can't exactly hide these, none of us are small. Even under a man's suit they will show through."

"I didn't say it was perfect, Hannah," sulked Heidi.

"That is stupid, Heidi," Petra chipped in from her bed.

"Wait, no she might have something here. Petra, hand me a couple of those bandages from the first aid kit in your bag."

"What are you thinking?"

"Just get them and come here. Now remove your blouse and stand with your arms up."

"This won't work, that's even more stupid than Heidi's suggestion."

"It will work. Heidi, hold this end under her armpit."

I continued to wrap the bandages tightly around Petra's chest; she then put her blouse back on. Although a little bulky, she no longer had any female curves.

"I stand corrected, Hannah. It looks okay actually - feels like I can't breathe though."

"Take short breaths then."

"Heidi? Can you go and purchase a suit and a hat big enough to hide her hair in, but not so that it will look out of place?"

Heidi returned after an hour or so. I replaced the bandages on Petra, and she got into the suit, put her hair up so it would sit in the top of the hat. She actually looked okay, a little feminine facially, but passable as a young man. Petra needed to practice her walk, so she spent the next few hours trying not to swing her hips. The trousers were a little baggy, so they did help to hide her hips and butt. Heidi and I went off to check on the courier and left Petra to her practising.

I placed my ear against his door, but I couldn't hear anything. He was either sleeping or had gone out. We needed to know, because if he wasn't in his room, it would be an ideal moment to search it. I motioned to Heidi to move out of sight, then simply knocked on the door. If he answered I was ready with a plausible reason for doing so - I would simply ask for Petra, a friend. There was no answer and so with Heidi now on watch duty I picked the lock and entered his room. I checked around his room just in case he was stupid enough to leave the diamonds lying around, but no. One thing I did find was his train ticket for Berlin and yes, he was booked on the next train out of Rome, tomorrow morning at 9am.

We returned to our room and Petra was ready, so she went down to the reception area and sat reading a paper and having a coffee, waiting for the courier to return so she could make eye contact with him. The best laid plans always have an unexpected twist. We were hoping he would return alone but he didn't; he still had the young man from earlier with him. Heidi and I watched as they collected his key and started up the stairs with Petra following them.

"I hope she doesn't do anything silly, Heidi. We need to stay here for another week yet."

"She knows that, Hannah. This improvisation stuff certainly keeps the heart thumping though!"

After several minutes passed Heidi and I climbed the two flights of stairs up to our room, expecting to see Petra—but there was no sign of her.

"Where can she be, Hannah? We didn't see her as we came upstairs."

"Let's check the courier's room, Heidi. It's the only place she can be."

Again, I placed my ear to his door and listened. I could hear shuffling and so I tapped on the door, it opened but only enough so the person on the inside could look out with one eye.

"It's us, Petra, let us in!"

"What have you done, Petra? This is going to bring the local police," Heidi stated, with more than a little terror in her voice.

She had killed them both, the young man with poison and the courier with a knife stab to the neck. Thinking quickly, the only way out of this was to stage the room, make it look like a joint suicide between lovers. Male homosexual relationships were frowned upon in Nazi Germany just as much as and in some cases more so than their hatred towards the Jews. They had sent many homosexual men to concentration camps, or simply shot them. This type of behaviour would not be tolerated under any circumstance.

I took my cyanide pill and placed it into the young man's mouth, crushing it. The knife was still in the courier's neck, so I instructed Petra and Heidi to strip him but be careful not to remove the knife. I stripped the young man and laid him on the bed, we then placed the courier beside him and placed the young man's hand on the knife. Crude, but effective.

We laid out fresh clothes for the courier and took the blood-soaked ones with us. We cleaned and searched the room for the diamonds. I was becoming more and more frustrated by the minute as there was no sign of them anywhere. We even checked the courier's suit just in case he had them sewn into the lining. It suddenly occurred to me that if the British could hide things in everyday objects, then why couldn't the Nazis?

"Check the false leg, Petra, but be careful," realising that was the only place we hadn't looked. This perhaps should have come to me sooner. The only reason they would allow a Nazi party member who was a cripple to stay on active duty was because he could be useful, and what better place to hide something of value?

The false leg removed, we peered inside, only to find what seemed to be padding, I removed it and checked it, but nothing was hidden.

"Do you think we have made a mistake, Hannah, and it was actually the other guy who was the real courier?" said Petra.

"No, this is our man, everything fits. What else can you see in there?"

Petra took a closer look at the now exposed wooden base and I watched as she thrust her hand down into it. As though in one single motion, she pulled it out again with an accompanying pop sound, like removing a cork from a bottle of wine. She now had hanging from a single finger the top of a hidden compartment. She looked inside again and turned it towards me. As it came into view, I saw some black cloth and reached inside to retrieve it. It was a pouch as big as the palm of my hand and it was full of something. I instructed Petra and Heidi to replace the false leg, complete the cleaning of the room and do it as quickly as possible. We took it in turns to leave the room and I locked it behind me.

Swiftly, and I have to say with excitement, I made my way back up the flight of stairs to our room were the other girls where now waiting. Petra was already changing back into her dress.

"What is in the pouch, Hannah, let's see what we have?" said Heidi excitedly.

I took the pouch and pulled on the string, and instantly my eyes were dazzled by the sparkling gems inside. I poured them out onto my bed and in total silence we just looked at them for what seemed to be hours, but in reality, was only a few seconds.

"We have no time to waste. Heidi, run us through the information you have collected about the villa?" I asked as I replaced the diamonds into the pouch.

"How much do you..." Petra began to say.

"Not now Petra, time is of the essence now. We have to get these diamonds out of here. Heidi, please continue."

"I have drawn up a small map of three different exit routes just in case. The villa itself is a secluded, two-storey building with balconies which, if required, can be used for escape. There is a small building approximately a quarter of a mile away which you can use as a staging area prior to pick up. The driver will drop you there on the morning of the 9th. It's all here for you Hannah, good luck."

"Right Heidi, you must go, we will meet you in Switzerland on the 10th. Firstly, we must split the diamonds up into smaller packages so you can hide them easier. It's going to be uncomfortable for you, but it's only for a day. Here are your travel documents, now get ready quickly."

"I am going to miss you girls."

"Stop with the soppy stuff, Heidi - get going! Remember, catch any train heading north, just get out of Rome today." I gave her a little hug and Petra offered a thumbs up and a smile as she left the room.

I opened the bottle of brandy which I had taken from the courier's room and took a couple of big drinks. My heart was racing, it had all been somewhat off the cuff, but we managed it despite the sloppy execution.

Several hours had passed and as Petra and I were getting ready to go and have dinner, I realised I still had the courier's room key.

"Crap, Petra. Look, I still have this," I said, showing her the room key for the courier's room.

"We have to get rid of that Hannah, and fucking quickly."

It also then occurred to me that the room would be locked from the inside, by the occupants, more so if they had the intention of committing suicide!

"What are you going to do Hannah? We can't be found with any connection to his room, I guess this shows we can't think of everything, every time." Petra was good at stating the obvious.

"Wait here for me. I will be back soon, don't leave the room Petra."

I quickly put the trousers and shoes on from the suit we had used earlier and made my way down to his room and snuck back in. I locked the door from the inside and opened the window. It was only one floor up; I could make it. Well, that's what I kept telling myself as I climbed out of the window, leaving it open to allow fresh air in, and onto the ledge that went around the building on every floor. I made my way around the building carefully and somewhat slowly, to be honest; this was my first time on the outside of a building. His room was on one side away from the front and ours at the back, but even so I had to be quiet, so I didn't alert anyone as I passed by any occupied rooms.

Finally, I was under our room. The building structure was such that I could use the large sized stone that protruded around each window as a kind of climbing frame. I could just get my fingers into the grooves between them, but my shoes at this point were useless so I kicked them off. Now, hanging on the windowsill of our room, I tapped on the window to get Petra's attention.

"What the fuck are you doing out there, Hannah?"

"Just help me in Petra!"

"I had to lock the door from the inside to help ensure that whoever found them would think it was suicide; the only way out was through the window."

"You could have told me what you were doing!"

"I didn't know when I left, I was making it up as I went along, Petra. Now, let's get some food."

The next day was filled with the unknown. Was the courier supposed to check out today? And if so, how long would it take before the bodies were found? We had to stay in the hotel, as checking the scene ourselves could be viewed as suspicious since we had booked our room until the 10th.

Chapter Eleven

The day continued to draw on, and as Petra and I sat in the reception area of the hotel having coffee late that afternoon, the place came alive with police. They must have finally found the bodies. We sat watching as the hotel staff and police frantically shuffled about. The police took and started checking the register book. One of them approached us and started asking questions.

"How long have you been staying here?"

"Since mid-December," I replied.

"When are you leaving?"

"The 10th of January."

"The purpose of your stay here?"

"Visiting relatives over the Christmas period, and taking in some of the sights of Rome."

"Your papers, please."

We handed over our papers, which we were sure would be fine as they had been so far. The names and addresses in Rome of our so-called relatives had been provided by the British, so everything should be okay, but this was still a moment of anxiety for me and Petra. We just had to stay calm and act as though we had nothing to worry about. After about ten minutes the officer returned and handed back our papers.

"Thank you. Ladies, please stay in the hotel until we give you permission to leave."

"What is going on?" I asked him.

"Two dead bodies have been found in one of the rooms and so we are checking everyone," he replied.

Things had suddenly become more complicated due to the local head of the SS arriving. I guess his presence was unavoidable due to the standing of the courier. He insisted on double checking everyone again; they simply didn't trust anyone. I think he was putting off going up to the room. The police officer asked him twice if he would go up there as they wanted to move the bodies, but couldn't until he had completed his investigation of the area. He stayed downstairs as long as he could. He finally couldn't put it off any longer and headed upstairs to the courier's room.

"Hannah, look, he has come straight back down."

"That means our plan has worked, he was obviously disgusted by what he saw and couldn't stay in the room, Heidi. Aren't they supposed to be heartless individuals?" I replied with a little condescending laughter.

"It also shows that our thoughts about the courier were correct, Hannah - not everyone knows who he is and what he was doing."

"We know just how untrusting the Nazis are, Petra, only two or maybe three high ranking SS officers would know exactly what he was doing. We are in the clear with this one."

"Yes, maybe Hannah, but one thing we haven't sorted out yet is how to turn the diamonds into cash."

"One thing at a time, Petra. I am sure Heidi will also be considering that factor and maybe she has already come up with a solution. Now let's go up to our room and run through the intel a couple more times just to be sure we are ready for the weekend."

We left the police to tidy up our mess. The SS officer didn't hang around, disgusted by what he saw, I guess. The Nazis really didn't like anyone that is gay, more so if that person was a member of their ranks.

We spent the next few days going over the layout of the villa, which was provided by the Italian underground, and studied the exit map produced by Heidi. Friday the 9th soon came around.

"Petra, get our stuff packed and ready to go, we will check out this morning and our driver will be here soon," I shouted from the bathroom.

"It's already done, Hannah, we're all ready to go."

We checked out of the hotel and walked outside where our driver was supposedly waiting for us. We saw a man get out of a car and stand in front of it; he then lit a cigar. That was the first part of the signal, and we walked over to him.

"Do you like the smell of cigars, ladies?" he asked.

"I prefer cigarettes," I replied, which was the confirmation that he was our man.

"Put your bags in the boot, we must go."

Petra got in the back and I sat in the front passenger seat.

"So, what are your names?" he asked.

"No names, that way if you're caught and tortured you can't give anything away."

"You think I would talk? I would rather die."

"Maybe." I wasn't going to debate his ability to resist torture. "Did you get us a couple of evening dresses?"

"Yes, they are at the safe house, which is only ten minutes away from the villa. You can stay there for the rest of the day until I come to collect you to take you to the villa at 20.00."

"Okay."

We spent the remainder of the day just sitting around, eating bread and fruit and a little meat that the Italian underground had provided for us, going over the plan, villa layout and all possible exit routes. The day seemed to go by quickly. Before I knew it, it was time to get cleaned up and dressed.

Our driver arrived at 20.00. It was only a few minutes to the villa, and the driver dropped us at the side entrance as we were not supposed to go in through the main one - it was reserved for dignitaries. Now all we had to do was find Ernst Heinrich, which shouldn't be too hard as we had seen a picture of him supplied by the British.

We blended in nicely, and it wasn't long before we were approached by several men. We had to play our parts, so we merely went with the flow for now. A small orchestra was playing and there seemed to be a never-ending flow of food and alcohol. Every room was full of people, seemingly enjoying themselves. I sat with a man in the bar whilst Petra was with another man in the dining room. Surely, our man should turn up to at least one of these two areas, food and drink, but it was now 22.30 and there was still no sign of him.

After about another hour I spotted him with one of the other girls entering the bar area, no sign of any guards with him though. I made an excuse to go to the toilet and en route I signalled to Petra that I had found him by placing my handbag under my left arm.

Petra implied to her man she wanted to go to his room with him now. She whispered in his ear what she was going to do to him, and a look of excitement engulfed his whole face. She needed to get rid of him and quickly, but also needed to get a look upstairs to find out the floor plan and if there were any guards up there. So, she led him up to his room and wasted no time satisfying him. Whilst this was happening, I kept a watchful eye on our target.

Thirty minutes later, Petra came back down and headed to the toilet, giving me a signal - a slight nod to follow her.

"I know which room he is staying in Hannah, up the stairs and turn right. You will see two guards at the end of the hall, they have to be his guards, right?"

"I will make contact with the target. He has been eyeing me up all night. Petra, you will need to look after my man; get him to take you upstairs."

"Use this red wine to spill on his current companion to get rid of her, Hannah."

As I walked back into the bar area, I approached the target. I took a false trip, spilling the whole contents of my glass all over his current companion. She instantly stood up, letting out a barrage of insults at me in Italian.

"Cazzo, puttana, stronzo!"

"I am so sorry, signorina, there is a bathroom just around the corner where you can clean up."

"Vaffanculo," she replied as she pushed past me and headed off to the bathroom.

Heinrich immediately stood up, and after listening to her insults and watching her storm off, he turned his attentions to me.

"Guten abend, fraulein, have you just arrived?" Heinrich asked me with a smile.

I had to think quickly to ensure I did not reply in German.

"Sorry, sir. I only speak Italian and English," I replied.

"Good evening, fraulein. Have you just arrived?" he asked again, but now in English.

"Good evening, sir. No, I have been here a while. It would be a pleasure to take care of you for the rest of the evening," I replied.

"What is your name, fraulein?"

"Sofia, sir," I replied as I gently kissed his neck.

It was almost midnight and now everyone was well under the influence of alcohol and getting into the full swing of the party—including Heinrich. All around us there were naked or half naked women with a slobbering drunken man attached in one form or another.

"Shall we go to your room, mein herr?" I asked him as I ran my hand down the inside of his thigh.

"Ja, Ja, let's go," he replied. He was so drunk I had to help him out of his chair and up the stairs. We turned right toward the guards and as we approached, he shouted at them to open the door. The guards gave the standard body bracing, clicking of the heels salute, and opened the door.

They looked at each other. "They are having so much fun, and there are certainly a lot of gorgeous girls here tonight," one said to the other.

They must have been able to hear the excitement in Heinrich's voice as I started working on him, undressing him whilst he laid on the bed.

"Do we have to stay here and listen to this?" One of the guards grumbled. Both now really wanted to get a piece of the action, but they were not supposed to leave their post. With that, the door down the hall opened and they both turned to look. It was Petra.

Petra

Completely naked, I stepped out into the hallway. Their eyes were fixated on me, and both were now as hard as concrete. I slowly walked toward them, stopping a few steps before.

"My man has collapsed in a drunken state before he could satisfy me; can one of you help me out please," I said, slowly moving towards the one on the right to press my naked body against his.

"You stay here, I will be back soon," he excitedly said to his comrade. "We can take turns, Ja? No one will know because Heinrich is busy getting his fill."

"Okay, but be quick, we don't want to get caught."

As he stepped toward my room, he asked, "What is your name?"

"Petra," I replied, with an inviting smile on my face, leading back to the room I was in. As we entered, he asked, "Where is the officer you came up here with?"

"Oh, he is in the bathroom, on the floor passed out," I replied.

He was actually in the bathroom, but not passed out. I had killed him with a perfect stab to his neck and the last thing he saw was me washing his blood off my body.

I start to undress the guard, kissing him all over and slowly moving my hands over his body. I unclipped his belt and dropped his trousers revealing his somewhat oversized manhood. To be honest, it was one of the biggest I had seen and so I decided I had to know what it felt like inside me. I pushed him onto the bed, teasing him with my body as I rubbed my silky soft skin against him, slowly making my way up his body and onto the bed. Now astride him, I backed myself up and inserted him into me. It was a little uncomfortable to start with and for a brief moment I forgot why I was there.

I soon returned to reality. I leaned forward and ran my hands through his hair, flipping the top of my ring. With a short but precise motion I hit him right on the main vein in his neck. The tension in his body increased immediately; every muscle felt like it was about to explode as he struggled for life. I stayed on top of him as I watched and felt the life drain out of him with some kind of morbid satisfaction that the last thing he felt, and saw was me.

I quickly covered him with a sheet and headed for the door. With a silenced pistol hiding behind my back, I opened the door, stepped out into the hallway and shouted for his comrade in a horrified voice,

"Something is wrong, he isn't moving! Come quickly!"

He hesitated for just a few seconds, then, seeing that I was certainly distressed, he rushed down to the room.

"What has happened?" he asked.

"We were just getting started, and he suddenly stopped breathing," I panted, feigning distress.

As he bent over to investigate his comrade; I put the pistol to his head and fired a single shot. That was my part completed. I quickly cleaned up, dressed and headed to Heinrich's room. I softly knocked on the door.

"Hannah, Hannah! It's me, open the door."

There was no reply and so I tried again, but still no sound. I was becoming little anxious. What had happened, had he killed her? These and many other thoughts start racing through my mind. I turned to head back to the room with the guards in to see if they had a door key but as I did so I heard her.

"Petra, Petra, quickly! Get in here!"

I turned back and there was Hannah at Heinrich's, door gesturing with a wave of her fingers to come in.

"I thought he had fucking killed you, Hannah!"

"I was in the bathroom cleaning up Petra."

"Do you have the paperwork?"

"No, I can't find the briefcase. Help me look."

We searched every single piece of furniture, inside and underneath drawers. We looked everywhere but there was no sign of it. Suddenly Petra shouted, "Found it!" It wasn't really hidden at all; it was simply on the coat hook under his over coat.

"Let's get the fuck out of here, my heart is pounding so much now I think it's going to explode in my chest," exclaimed Petra.

We climbed down the outside of the building to the waiting driver. We got in the back seat and let out a massive sigh of relief, then hugged each other for a short while.

"Did you get it?" the driver asked. "Girls, did you get it?" he repeated.

"Yes, we did," we both said simultaneously.

"Now let's get the hell fuck out of here before we have the whole German and Italian armies coming after us," ordered Petra.

"Okay ladies, it's time for some *evasion* techniques," grinned the driver as he pulled away, spinning the wheels on the gravel drive.

Petra and I changed our clothes as the driver headed towards the Swiss border. He wasn't taking us all the way, just far enough away from the area so that we could catch a train to Switzerland at a northern station, Florence or Bologna perhaps.

We drove through the night and arrived at Florence around 07.30. The driver dropped us off. He stated that we needed to change our mode of transportation; we should take the bus to Bologna and then the train from there to Milan.

Both of us were very tired and so we tried to catch as much sleep as we could on the bus. Just after lunch time we were dropped off at the train station in Bologna. It was swamped with German soldiers, travelling to and from the southern areas of Italy.

The train ride to Milan was uneventful, everyone just went about their normal activities. I couldn't help but wonder what was happening at the villa now, they must have found the bodies! Hopefully, it would be total mayhem.

We exited the station and headed for the arranged meeting place to link up with our transportation into Switzerland. A black-market trader who made regular trips in and out of Switzerland to trade Italian food for dairy products, which he would then take into Germany to sell.

The Swiss, although not directly involved in the war, still had their own problems. They feared an invasion from Germany, so they fortified their northern borders, including those over the Alps. Since 1939 the Swiss Nazi party had made several attempts to disrupt the government with several high-ranking political members falling on the side of the Axis powers. Most of the country's food and fuel came in via crucial rail lines from Germany, France and Italy and due to the war, the country was economically affected but it stood fast as an independent country and seemed to be holding its own.

Although the German newspapers kept the population informed of current affairs, and in particular the country's war achievements, it had to be said they reported from a one-sided point of view. One of the positive aspects of joining the British was that as part of our mission brief. We got background information providing us with a much more informed, balanced overview.

We arrived at the café on the outskirts of Milan where we were meeting our contact. We would be travelling with him as his daughters, and to help unload and load the truck.

"He is late, Hannah."

"Yes, Petra, I can tell the time, just keep your eyes open for the truck," I replied, as I finished my coffee.

A middle-aged man approached our table and sat down. He took a few moments to look us both over, and then he spoke.

"The rain in the Alps falls mainly as snow."

"But come Spring, it turns back to water," I replied, which was our new introduction code phrase.

"Come, we are late and have to get moving, the truck is around the corner," he stated as he stood up.

We got in the truck and, there, he passed us some clothes.

"You must change, you have to at least dress like truck driver's mates," he stated as he started the engine and drove off.

"How far is it to the border?" I wanted to know.

"About two hours," he replied, adding, "You can stash your bags behind the seat." Which we did, but we kept our pistols in a handy to reach place.

"You will not need those," as he watched us both hide our pistols in our clothing.

"We like to be ready for anything," was my firm response.

"We shouldn't have any problems at the border, I make this trip twice a week and the guards at the border are used to seeing me now. Besides, I always give them that parcel under your seat."

I looked under the seat to find a box filled with all kinds of food items from Italy.

"A bribe?" raising an eyebrow.

"An incentive, but I am not sure what they will make of you two."

"Don't worry about us, we can take care of ourselves," said Petra.

"Do you know if a friend of ours got into Switzerland okay a few days ago?" I asked him.

"Couldn't tell you. We act independently. That way we can't give anyone up if we are caught," he answered.

An hour later we arrived at the border crossing and our driver started hitting the steering wheel and mumbling under his breath.

"What is wrong?" I asked him.

"They have changed the guards," he Muttered.

"What? So, what's the plan?" I asked, not liking that he seemed nervous.

"We will have to play it by ear, follow my lead," he ordered.

As we approached the guards, I looked around to see if there were more of them but couldn't see anyone. One of them was on the left by the little hut, another on the right who operated the barrier, with the third manning a machine-gun just on the other side facing towards the Swiss border.

"Be ready," I whispered to Petra, who acknowledged by tapping her pistol.

"Halt!" one of the guards shouted. "Papers, please. What are you carrying?" he asked the driver.

"Produce for Switzerland, here are my papers," our driver replied.

"Out, everyone out," the guard barked at us all.

At gunpoint they forced us all to the back of the truck and asked our driver to open it. I could feel this wasn't going well, and so I gave Petra a simple nod. Pulling our silenced pistols out we quickly shot them both in the head – quick and effective.

"Petra, sneak around and take out the soldier at the machine gun post, you help me get rid of these two in this ditch."

The driver was in shock at how suddenly we had taken these two guards out. He seemed frozen to the spot, so I slapped him in the face.

"Hey, come on! We have to move them," I said. "Grab his legs. Come on, grab his legs," I repeated frantically.

We moved the bodies into the ditch and headed back to the truck. Having taken care of the third guard, Petra was waiting with the barrier raised. We drove through and she dropped it behind us.

The driver didn't speak another word for the rest of our journey. I guess he couldn't believe that two relatively young girls could kill with such efficiency and speed. He couldn't wait to get rid of us, and so he dropped us off at the next village with a train station.

"That didn't quite go to plan, Hannah."

"No, but we must get to Zurich. Come on, let's see when the next train north is leaving."

With a little over five hours to wait for the next train, we changed into warmer clothing and I reminded Petra of our current situation.

"Remember, although we are now out of occupied Italy and Switzerland is neutral, there is still danger here. This country is full of Nazi sympathisers and spies. Be careful."

"I know that, Hannah. I am not fucking stupid you know, you don't have to remind me," she replied.

"I am just making sure we blend in from now on, and there's no more trouble," seeking to placate any ruffled feelings.

Chapter Twelve

It took us a couple of days to travel up to Zurich, changing trains several times. It was completely uneventful and felt strange in some ways. The only thing the train staff were interested in was if we had a valid ticket - not once did we get asked for our papers. It was a different world entirely, like a dream almost. The Swiss people were friendly and helpful, and there were no signs of the raging war surrounding the country. People were free to travel and go about their business as usual, like I could only imagine a country free from war behaved.

Petra and I exited the train station and headed for the Excelsior hotel where Heidi should have been waiting.

"We have been here for several hours Hannah, and there is no sign of Heidi."

"To be honest I am not sure where she can be, Petra."

"You don't think she has left us and taken the diamonds for herself, do you?"

"Don't be silly Petra, she wouldn't do that to us. Besides you know how she is, she's a worrier."

"I just think something isn't right," looking around, hoping for a sign.

"And you are always looking on the bad side of things. She is probably out walking."

"I will ask at reception which room she is in."

"Good idea, and then you should go up and knock on her door, just in case she is in her room."

Petra returned, shaking her head. "She isn't in her room, and the receptionist hasn't seen her all day."

We sat for the rest of the day in the reception area, drinking coffee and waiting for Heidi to show up, but she never did. Before returning to our room for the night I asked the receptionist to leave her a message for when she returned.

I was beginning to agree with Petra; something wasn't right. Heidi should have been there, but I wasn't going to tell her that. We were meeting Falcon in the morning to hand over the intelligence we got from the villa, and he would ask where she was if she didn't return. I wasn't sure what I was going to tell him!

"You don't think she has been captured by the Swiss Nazi party, do you Hannah?"

"Why would that happen, Petra? You're just making stuff up. They have no idea who they are looking for, so why would they take her? Now shut up and go to sleep."

The next morning, we were woken by someone knocking at our door at 06.30.

"Hello," I shouted, as I climbed out of bed and walked towards the door, clutching my pistol in readiness.

Two more knocks at the door.

"Who is it?" I asked.

A soft voice I instantly recognised. "It's me, open the door." Placing my pistol down on the table close to the door, I then unlocked it and finally saw the smiling face of Heidi.

"Where the hell have you been? Get in here!" I must have said this with anger as her faced dropped the smile and turned to shock.

"I've been..." she started to say, but I interrupted her.

"Do you know how worried we have been Heidi? Why didn't you leave a message, are you okay?"

Heidi reacted by standing firmly, hands on hips. "If you shut up for a moment, I will tell you. Yes, I am fine."

"Were you captured?" Petra chipped in.

"No, now will you both stop with the questions so I can tell you what I have been doing?" she continued, "It occurred to me whilst travelling up here that we need someone to sell the diamonds to, as we can't sell them anywhere in Europe because it will attract too much attention, right?"

"Yes," Petra and I replied in unison.

"Okay. So, I remembered a Swiss industrialist using Madam Kitty's salon, his regular girl telling me that he and his wife travel all over the world on business and that some of that business wasn't entirely legal."

"Go on; you have our attention now," I interjected with eager anticipation in my voice.

"While waiting around for you girls to arrive I thought it might be a clever idea to track them down, so I have been making enquires. They live just outside

Zurich. Although I haven't made contact yet, I have been to their house."

"You still could have left some kind of fucking message for us Heidi, we didn't know what was going on and we began to worry, didn't we Hannah?" Petra piped up. I nodded in agreement.

"Right, look girls, we will have to leave this for now. We need to get ready to go and meet Falcon."

Later that morning we sat in a café awaiting the arrival of Falcon. He was late, or so we thought. Another forty minutes passed by and finally he arrived.

"You are late," I said, in a challenging tone.

"Now, do you have the information?" he asked, ignoring my statement.

"Yes, we have it," I replied as I passed over the envelope to him.

"Good job. I will get this over to HQ for them to analyse."

"What is next for us?" I asked.

"We're now blanket bombing most of the major cities in Germany so you can't return there and resume your cover, that much is for sure."

"I don't want to return to Germany, the thought of being bombed again scares the crap out of me to be honest," I replied.

"Look, Hannah, you will go wherever HQ sends you, but I understand what you're saying. It's entirely up to them what happens next, but first things first, we need to find you somewhere to stay that is safe."

"I have an aunt that lives in Austria, we could stay with her for a while," offered Heidi.

"Good idea. You go there, I will contact you in a few days," and, making a note of the address, Falcon left.

"You didn't tell me you had an aunt in Austria, Heidi?" I remarked.

"Yes, she lives with my parents actually. I didn't want to give him too much information, Hannah. Anyway, it's the closest place to Switzerland I could think of, just in case you wanted me to continue with the industrialist?"

"Always thinking well ahead Heidi, good move. We need to offload these diamonds as soon as possible, we can't be caught with them," I replied.

We headed off to pack and prepare for the journey to Austria. The journey out of Switzerland was easier than the one in, but I guess that was due to us being German and female. The Swiss would intern anyone they thought were soldiers, spies and even refugees due to their neutrality in this war. As German women, we were looked at less as a threat and so could travel about much more easily.

Soon enough we arrived in Feldkirch, Austria near the Swiss border. During our journey Heidi told me and Petra more about her family.

Heidi

"My family have not seen me for several years now; they have no idea where I am or what I am doing. I was enrolled in a boarding school in my late teenage years which later was turned in one of the Nazi schools for girls when the Nazi party came into total power."

"So, like me, you became lost in the system then?" asked Hannah.

"Yes. As you know, you're not allowed any contact with anyone while at those schools. I am looking forward to seeing my Mutter and vater again. I have often wondered to myself what happened to my sister; she was 12 years old when she left back in 1937."

We arrived at my hometown and made the short walk to my family house. I stood for a few minutes across the road, just staring at the house. I started to recall all the wonderful memories I had of being brought up here. I couldn't wait any longer, I knocked on the door and wait for a reply. After what seemed an hour but was only less than a minute the door swung open. A grey-haired lady stood staring back at me who I recognised, but not as my Mutter, it was my aunt.

"Hello, can I help you?" she said.

"Auntie, it's me, Heidi!"

"Oh, oh, oh my child, come in, come in! You have changed so much I hardly recognised you," Auntie replied.

My auntie had always been a robust kind of lady, stern-faced but with a soft caring voice, but you could see she was no stranger to inner pain. It showed in her eyes, caused by the loss of her husband and two elder brothers during the First World War.

The inside of the house had not really changed at all, apart from it felt noticeably quiet. I recalled that there always used to be music playing and the sound of laughter echoing around the house.

"These are my friends, Auntie. Hannah and Petra."

"This is still your home Heidi. You can bring anyone you wish with you. Nice to meet you both," she replied.

"Auntie, where are my parents?" The house felt empty.

"I am sorry, but they have passed, two years ago now. When they lost contact with you, they started searching but to no end. Then the Nazis also took your sister to one of those horrid schools for Nazi girls. The strain on them was too much to bear; they had lost both of you. They... they killed themselves a few months later."

My eyes filled up with tears and ran down my cheeks like unstoppable waterfalls. I couldn't believe it. This situation only added to the hatred I already felt towards the Nazis and I had to hold it inside as I didn't want to upset my auntie. We were now the only family we had left. My aunt kept hold of me from the time I arrived—it felt like nothing could hurt me, I was safe and had nothing to worry about.

"What happened to my sister?"

"She was taken not long after you, I have no idea where, Heidi."

"She is now in the system, so she could be anywhere, Auntie."

"At least one of you has found your way home. Who knows, maybe your sister will too."

"Is it ok if we stay with you for a few days, Auntie?"

"Of course, it is, you don't need to ask Heidi. It's so nice to see you again, I thought you were lost forever."

"Let's have some tea and then if you don't mind, I would like to visit my parents at the cemetery, Auntie."

"But of course, my child, I will take you."

"I will freshen up. Which room can I use?"

"Your room, it's still there just as you left it. Your friends can use your sister's room."

As we made our way upstairs, Hannah and Petra kept stopping to look at family photos taken in my early years.

"I am sorry about your parents Heidi," Hannah consoled.

"Thank you, Hannah. Well, now all I have is my aunt and you two."

"We will always be here for you, Heidi. Would you prefer we found a hotel to stay in, to give you time alone with your aunt?" asked Petra.

"No, please stay, it will be better if you stay." I wanted them close to me. It felt unbelievable that Hannah and Petra could and would be so compassionate towards another human being. After all, I had only ever seen their darker sides. I guess they must have known how I was feeling as they had both gone through this grief already.

I showed them to my sister's room, and we freshened up and changed.

"Heidi, what do we call your aunt? You never did tell us her name," asked Hannah.

"Oh, just call her auntie. She has a strange, totally unpronounceable long name, so everyone calls her Auntie."

We all made our way back downstairs and Auntie had prepared some food and tea for us. It wasn't much, a little cold chicken and bread.

"How did you get those scars on your face, Heidi?" she asked whilst pouring the tea.

"We got caught up in the bombing of Berlin Auntie. Hannah almost died. It was horrible."

"Berlin, and what were you doing in Berlin? Is that where you worked?" she asked.

I had to think quickly here. I couldn't tell her the truth - it would destroy her.

"We all worked as administration assistance for the Reich, collecting and sorting documents. Boring, really," Hannah chipped in.

"Yes, and the building we worked in was bombed by the Allies. In fact, they bombed everything. The city is in ruins, Auntie, so I suggested coming down here to get away from it all once we could all travel."

"Hitler, he promised so much and has only brought death to many countries and their people," replied Auntie.

"No one can escape, so many countries and so many people all now bound together by one common denominator—loss. And all because of one man," growled Hannah.

"It's best not to dwell on the past, it can consume you. We are all still alive, we must look to the future girls," stated Auntie.

"Yes, Auntie, that's what we are trying to do," I replied.

"Come, Heidi, let's go and visit your parents. You girls can stay here if you wish."

"I think we will have a walk around the town whilst you visit your parent's graves, Heidi. We will catch you later," offered Hannah.

Auntie and I took the ten-minute walk up to the cemetery, and of course I knew instantly that Hannah and Petra were in fact surveying the town and taking stock of their surroundings, just in case!

Hannah

"I have been thinking, Petra. Maybe we should leave Heidi here with her aunt. She can continue with finalising the selling of the diamonds."

"Okay, but what are we going to do? Falcon told us to stay here and wait for him to contact us."

"Yes, and we should give him a few days to do exactly that. We have collected a vast amount of information over the past and it shouldn't go to waste Petra."

"You're suggesting we hit our own targets, Hannah?"

"Yes, but we could also use the same techniques that we used whilst evacuating Berlin. Kill as many high-ranking officers as we can as we move around."

"We would have to be careful with that, a trail of dead officers would soon lead them to us. Don't you think it's better to just target a few specific officers, those of strategic importance for that area?"

"You might be right Petra," I considered. "But let's also not forget what happened in Prague when the resistance there killed Heydrich—the Germans responded by massacring a whole village."

"I had forgotten about that. So, what is the best plan?"

"I think it's best to not discriminate; a German soldier is a German soldier. The more that are dead, the fewer are left to fight against the Allies. We could also look at the many collaborators we know of."

"Let's sit and have a cup of tea and try to formulate some kind of plan. We certainly can't wait for the British; it could take weeks before we hear anything, and that isn't why we started this. We are supposed to be killing Germans! Not sitting on our ass for weeks at a time!"

"I agree, but whatever we come up with, we have to consider, Heidi."

We spent the next few hours just watching the world go by and drinking tea. Although, to be honest, I was actually thinking mostly about moving on and getting back into the fight and I think I may well have got the perfect formula. Now all I had to do is run it by the girls – oh, and Falcon.

We headed back to Heidi's. Petra could tell I was in deep thought and so we didn't speak at all during our walk back. Upon arriving back at Heidi's, her aunt had prepared some food -goulash- and it smelled great and tasted wonderful. In fact, I had forgotten what real home cooking was like. Each mouthful was a delight to the taste buds.

After dinner I sat for a while, running through our next move in my head. What was required? Would there be any possible reprisal from the Reich? - but then it occurred to me. This is war, and people die. In fact, thousands die every day. Taking out the odd German here and there wasn't really making much of a difference. Sure, everyone counted, but this one had to make a statement, something with a true impact! However, if this plan was going to work then there were a couple of things I needed to do.

I didn't sleep much that night and Heidi was the first to rise in the morning. Over a little bread and fruit, I told her I had to leave for a couple of days, which sparked an inevitable list of questions.

"Where are you going?"

"Heidi, at this time there is no point in telling you anything. If I can't secure what we need then my plan will not even get off the ground."

"Why are you going alone?"

"It's a one-person job, no need for all of us to risk travelling at this stage. Besides, you have a task that requires your attention, you need to move the diamonds - and quickly."

"What about Petra?"

"She can help you. I will return in two days. Oh, and contact Falcon and request a meeting for when I return. All will be revealed then."

"Hannah. I wish you would tell me what you are up to and where you're going." A look of concern and pleading in her eyes.

"Just focus on your objectives, Heidi, I've got this."

I immediately left for the train station and bought a ticket to the north of Austria. I was heading for Zell Am Moos, a small village near a lake. On the outside it appeared no different from any other Austrian lakeside village, but I knew its dark secret and it was crucial that I got my hands on some of it.

Several hours, a few train changes and two bus rides later, I arrived at my destination. I had travelled light and didn't want to attract any attention, so I didn't bother booking into a hotel. In fact, I had no intention of staying in the area longer than I had to. This was a hit and run job - well, more like a hit, drop and then run job. I didn't want nor need to travel with any of this stuff, all I needed to do was secure some of it and hide it for a later pick up.

I sat in a café and waited for darkness to fall. My target wasn't too far away and not very well guarded, or so I was told back in Berlin. A previous client at the brothel had told me about his very mundane job. The mainstream German soldier wanted to serve the Fuhrer body and soul; they hated any duty that didn't involve direct fighting. This client was quite angry with his assignment - guard duty at a German stockpile cave, in a little village with nothing going on.

He went on for hours in a non-stop, drunken soap box style. In fact, he went on so much that he got himself so worked up he forgot about why we were there. Even the sight of me naked wouldn't shut him up. I have to be honest; it did cross my mind that I had lost my attractiveness and for a while it began to get to me, but I soon came round and realised that sometimes they just needed to sound off and not get off. His loss.

It was time to move. It took me about twenty minutes to walk up to the cave. There was only one approach and that was straight ahead; one entrance and so no other way in. I hid in the trees for some time, watching the movements of the solitary guard. There was a little wooden cabin and a barrel outside with a fire burning. He was right, they must be bored to hell with nothing to do but listen to the radio and watch the night go by.

I took my coat off and ripped open my blouse, showing just enough to get his attention. I then began to run towards the cabin shouting "HELP!" repeatedly.

"HALT!" the guard shouted as he emerged from the cabin, pointing his rifle at me.

"Please help, he is trying to rape me!" I shouted back, slowly moving forward into the light from his fire, hoping once he saw me his instincts would kick in and he would try to protect me.

"Come, come," he shouted, waving his hand toward himself but now scanning the darkness behind me for my pursuer.

"Thank you, thank you! Is he out there?" I asked the soldier in a scared voice, whilst hiding behind him.

As he peered forward to look for my artificial attacker, I slipped the cap off my ring and struck him in the neck; he was down within seconds. I grabbed his key to the gate and entered the cave. There were many rooms to this cave, some with steel doors and some without. I found what I was looking for, grabbed several tins and locked it all back up, replaced the keys on the guard's body, got my coat and got out of there.

Because I only needed a small amount of this stuff, they wouldn't even notice it had gone. In fact, they would think the guard just died of natural causes or something, clean and tidy. Now to hide my loot in the lake for an easy pick up later.

I used a plastic bag and some rocks to weigh it down and placed the bag in the water a few steps out from the shore. I marked a tree with my knife so I could find it later. I got dressed and put on a fresh blouse from my bag.

I headed back into town and looked around for a vehicle, I needed to get out of there. It wasn't late in the evening, only around 22.00. The place was like a ghost town. My client was right again, there was nothing happening. It was easy to steal a car.

I drove through the night to Salzberg to catch the train back to Heidi's. I had to wait around for a few hours, so found a quiet spot to get some food. By lunch time, I was back and as I walked toward Heidi's home, I saw that Petra was stood on the front porch. She didn't look happy.

"What is going on, Hannah?" Petra started, even before I had stepped foot on the porch.

"All will be revealed, Petra, just wait until Falcon arrives," I replied.

"We don't have secrets, Hannah, where have you been?"

"Oh Petra, you're just bitchy because I went alone, and you don't like missing out."

"We are in this together, Hannah; you need to remember that."

"I am fully aware of that, Petra. I am not keeping you or Heidi out of this, it's just that what I had to do only took one person. You will love my plan; you're playing a major part in it. Just be patient so I don't have to repeat myself, Falcon should be here later today or tomorrow."

Petra just mumbled something under her breath, and I guessed it wasn't very pleasant. I was ready for a cup of coffee and to find out how Heidi got on with the diamonds.

"So, I just saw Petra on the front porch, she isn't in a very good mood, Heidi."

"No, she hasn't been since you left, totally bitchy. How did your trip go then?"

"Yes, it went as planned, Heidi. All will be revealed once Falcon arrives. How are we doing regarding the diamonds?"

Chapter Thirteen

Heidi

I visited the Keller's. I decided I would pose as the daughter of someone he knew who had died and say that I was there to invite them to the funeral. The chances of him remembering me from the brothel were very slim; he had never met me, but just to be sure I was wearing a wig and glasses.

I brought Hannah up to speed on my venture. "I have to be honest, Hannah, I was a little shaky when I knocked on their door. They have servants, and one of the biggest houses I have ever been in. They are nice people, but I soon realised that Mr Keller wasn't the man for the job. He's only interested in business, he spent most of his time on the phone.

"I spent most of my time talking to Mrs Keller, I realised very quickly she was one of those bored housewife types, and afternoon tea was the highlight of her day, so I decided to probe her further.

"Mrs Keller, or Daphne as she told me to call her, was in dire need of some liberation and excitement in her life. They certainly have no love for the Nazis, that is for sure. Mr Keller is only interested in money and doesn't care where it comes from.

"They travel all over the world for his business, but it would seem the only time they actually spend any time together is on the plane. She goes shopping, plays cards to fill her days - she is bored. I have her phone number now and we are developing a friendship; you can't rush this, Hannah."

Hannah had listened patiently. "Maybe not, but we need to move these diamonds and soon."

"Look, I am building on it. I am going to ring her again and visit for another day."

"Make that your only objective; there's nothing else for you to do but move those diamonds on."

"But what about......."

Hannah cut my sentence short. "You can help me with the planning, but we need you to concentrate on the diamonds, Heidi, please."

The front door opened and in walked Petra, with Falcon right behind her.

"Afternoon, ladies. Now, what is so important that you need to see me so soon?"

Hannah

"I have a plan that will give the Nazis a taste of their own medicine."

"You're supposed to be resting and waiting for London to go through the intelligence you gathered, not planning new missions, Hannah."

"We can't, and quite frankly won't, sit around doing nothing. Anyway, I have already completed phase one."

"So, without permission, you have already moved on with your plan? This will not do, Hannah. You're supposed to pass any plans through me to be sanctioned."

"What do you think you're here for now, to sanction the plan?"

"Honestly, you girls will be the death of me." He sighed mock dramatically." Alright, give me the overview."

"We all know that the Nazis are using poison gas to murder thousands of people, right?" Everyone just nodded in agreement. "Well, I know the location of one of their stockpiles of that gas, and I now have a few cans of it stored in a safe place, ready for pickup."

"You have my attention," stated Falcon, any fake boredom gone. Heidi and Petra both moved in closer with that eager look in their eyes.

"From our time in the brothels we know several locations in France where the Nazis have what they term 'weekend retreats', large chateaus that on any given weekend are full of officers of all ranks. They, of course, have contingency plans for air raids – cellars, to be exact, with steel bomb doors."

"How do we get them all in the shelter at the same time then?" asked Petra.

"Falcon, is it possible for, say, a single aircraft to drop a few bombs near one of these sites, to scare the officers into the cellar?" Heidi asked.

"Yes, that could be done, but bomb shelters are by their nature locked from the inside, so how do you stop them from getting out?"

"And how do you get the gas in, Hannah?" Petra wanted to know.

"Explosive charges placed on the ceiling directly above the door, that will bring the ceiling down to prevent anyone opening the door. Petra, they have to have air, there must be air vents somewhere!"

"Sounds like this could be done Hannah. What do you need from me?" Falcon was intrigued now.

"Can you get in touch with the French resistance? Heidi has a contact. She will give you the details. We will need a detailed plan of the chateau and surrounding area. We also require transport and say, twenty men to help with mopping up any soldiers that are not in the shelter."

"I will send you the intelligence via one of our F sections circuits in France. Expect them in a few days. They will also provide you with the resistance contact information."

As Falcon left, he bumped into Heidi's aunt returning from visiting a friend. This provoked a few questions that we were hoping to avoid.

"What is really going on, Heidi? Who was that man?"

"Auntie, don't worry he is our boss from Berlin, he called in to see how we were doing and if we needed anything."

Auntie walked round each of us in turn and gave us a hug, one of those parental hugs that makes you feel safe and then headed off upstairs.

"Right, Heidi, let's get to work. We are limited until we get the plans of the chateau, but we can work out our travel and escape plan. The French resistance will provide us with explosives and transport out."

"Petra, can you clean and prepare our best dresses? We're going to need them."

"Yes, Hannah. Finally, we are doing something which will make them think, pay back. This is great,

Hannah, the big one." Petra as she went off upstairs, sounded so happy.

"I do worry about Petra, the only time you really see her smile is when she is about to kill people."

"Oh, Heidi, she is okay. She is just passionate about ridding the world of the evil that is plaguing it. Now, what is the best route into France?"

"The fastest route is through Switzerland, but I think you're better off going through northern Italy – there's less hassle for you that way."

While waiting for the chateau plans, Heidi and I planned our escape route, secondary escape route and Petra got everything else ready - clothes, side arms cleaned and loaded, rings prepared with poison.

A couple of days later, around 04.00, I woke up and went downstairs for a glass of water. I needed to take some more pills. I was just about to switch on the light when...

"Leave the light off and don't move," a female voice from the darkness said in a quiet soft voice, whilst cocking back the hammer on her pistol.

"Who are you and what do you want?" I replied.

"What is your name?" she asked.

"Hannah. Again, what do you want?"

"Good, I have the right house then. Slowly, turn on the light and keep your voice down."

"Who are you?" I asked again. As I turned on the light, I saw a well-kept young lady sitting in the armchair, still pointing her pistol at me.

"Falcon sent me, I have the information you requested."

"If Falcon sent you then, *do you have some makeup I could borrow*?"

"*I only carry lipstick - after all, that's all a good woman needs.*"

"*That depends on the woman.*"

"The British and their silly first contact phrases, I wish they would come up with something with a little more kick," she said, as she put away her pistol.

"I will go and wake the others. Put the kettle on. Oh, and what do we call you?"

"I will not be staying long enough for any of that, maybe next time," she replied as she stood up and headed towards the kitchen.

I hastily woke the others and we returned to the kitchen.

"Here are the plans you requested. Now, they are very crude, but will give you enough information about the chateau for your purpose. The resistance has provided all the equipment you will require including gas masks, and..." she paused, like she didn't want to tell us.

"What?" I asked.

"Um... a little snag, nothing too major, I think. The British want you to proceed with your plan this weekend, I will be sending a plane to pick you up on Friday evening and you're to drop into France by parachute that same night."

"That's two days from now!" Petra, always ready to state the obvious.

"Why this weekend, and why parachutes?" I asked her.

"Sorry, I don't know the details. I was only given the information I have told you," She replied, as she put her hat on in preparation to leave.

"This just isn't on." Heidi turned to me. "How we can do this in such a brief time, Hannah?"

"Look girls, it's going to be rough enough - Petra and I have to jump out of an aeroplane, at night. We have two days to get this planned out, Heidi, so let's stop hanging onto the negatives and get this sorted. Now, let's look at the floor plan."

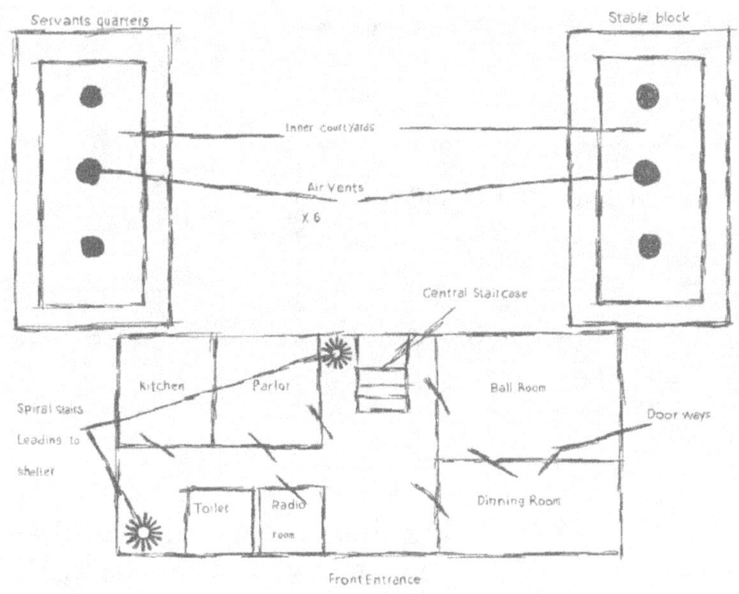

"We get the RAF to bomb the outskirts of the chateau to scare everyone down into the shelter. But what if they drop bombs on the chateau? It's going to be dark; how will they know what they are bombing?" Heidi raised an important question.

"Heidi, it's quite simple really. As soon as they hear the plane coming, they will turn off all the lights. Standard procedure, yes?"

"Okay," she nodded.

"We have someone on the roof with lights to show our position, thus providing the RAF with a beacon to stay away from. A few seconds before the plane is due to arrive, Petra or I will take out the radio room. Step one, inside the chateau."

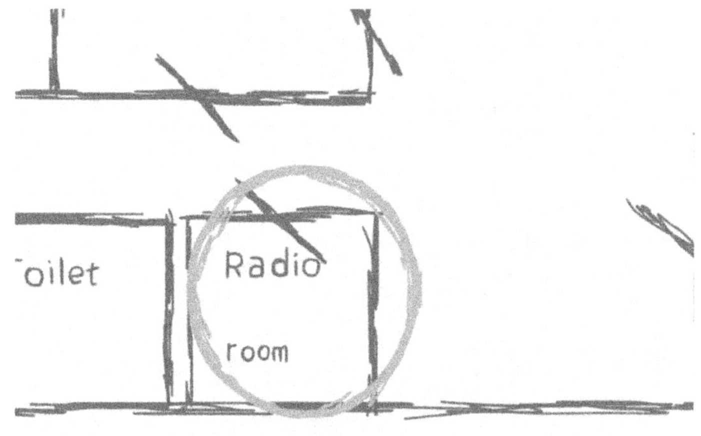

"As soon as the lights go out, the French resistance will enter, causing even more chaos. They will think they are under complete attack. There should only be a maximum of say, sixty people there, so it will not take long for them to get down into the shelter using both the staircases marked here on the map."

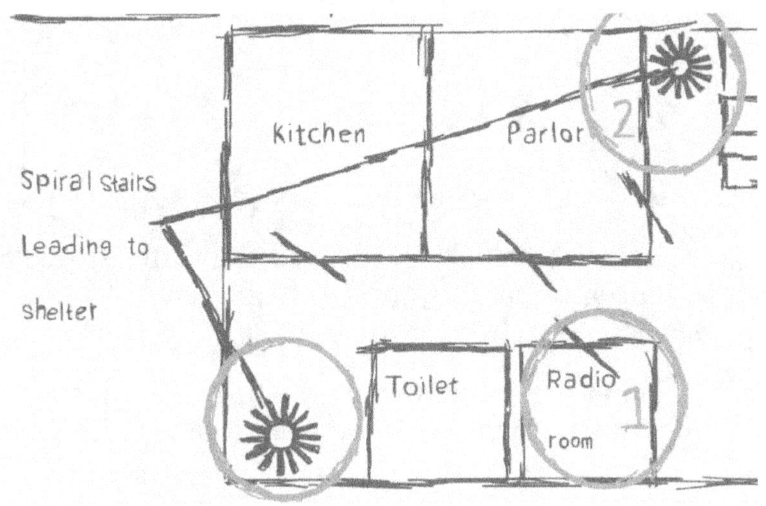

Heidi tapped a finger on the plan. "Once they are all inside, we blow the ceiling above the door to block it and stop them getting out. We also blow up both the spiral stair cases as a secondary measure."

"Yes, good thinking, Heidi." I had been about to say that but it was important to let Heidi take credit. I continued, "While we are doing that the resistance will be checking all the rooms just in case anyone is left. They will also round up the French servants and get them out of the area."

"What will I be doing, Hannah?" asked Petra.

"It would be best if we stick together. Petra, you can watch my back as I plant the explosives. Then we will move outside, to the vents."

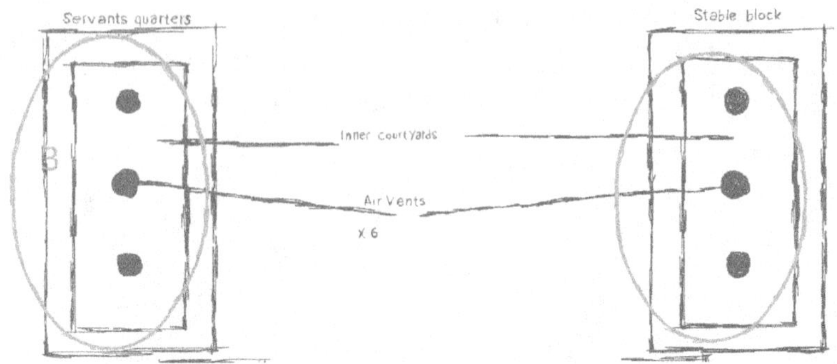

"You then block up three of the vents, drop the gas down the remaining three, block them off so none can escape and wait for it to do its job," finished Heidi.

"What are we going to do while we wait for the gas to work, Hannah? How long will it take to kill them all?"

"They can't get out. No one will be there to rescue them. We steal anything we can find that's light enough to carry - cash, jewellery, anything small, depending on its weight. It will take around four to six minutes until death occurs; they'll either crush each other in panic or die from lack of oxyen. So girls, I have to go and get the gas. I will be back later today."

"While you do that, Hannah, I will go over the plan again and make sure we haven't forgotten anything." Heidi being a perfectionist.

Before we knew it, Friday was here. I for one wasn't looking forward to a night jump. We had received parachute training back when we were all trained by the Nazis, but basic parachute training did not include night jumps so this would be the first time for both of us. I felt somewhat apprehensive about the whole thing.

Heidi was up early and on her way to visit Mrs Keller. We were all hoping for some good news from that visit, but only time would tell. Petra and I went over the plan again so we had it in our heads. Heidi had marked off the positions for the resistance fighters, both on the roof of the chateau and around the surrounding area. She had them encircling the chateau all with torches forming a ring of light, so the RAF had a clear picture of where not to bomb. All we needed now was clear skies!

"Hannah, I have to say that there is only one thing I have any concern about. Jumping at night scares the hell out of me."

"I feel the same way, Petra, but at least we are jumping into an open field surrounded by forest. The French resistance will be waiting for us, so if we get caught up in the trees they will be there to cut us down."

"That doesn't make me feel any calmer. Landing in trees is dangerous; this whole thing could be over before it starts."

"It's best to try and not think about it Petra. Now, let's go and get ready and make our way to the airstrip for pick up."

Nightfall was upon us and Petra and I waited at what we thought was the airstrip. It was pitch black; we couldn't see a thing. Seemingly from nowhere, the echoes of an aeroplane engine filled the night sky. Then, suddenly, the dark field turned into a brightly lit landing strip. The resistance were masters at this, waiting until the last possible moment to light their torches and get into position.

The plane landed and we hurried to get on board. In less than two minutes we were back in the air and on our way, These pilots were a breed to behold; specially trained and fearless individuals with a large side order of crazy.

Petra and I hardly spoke a word for the two hour flight - we both knew what was going through the other's mind!

Chapter Fourteen

Earlier that same day

Heidi

I arrived at the Keller's home for my second meeting with Daphne. We sat in the garden taking tea and chatting the day away. I decided it was time to push a little and finally find out if Daphne was up for the challenge ahead.

"How would you feel about adding some excitement to your life? No one will get hurt and you could make some real money, Daphne."

"I am always looking for excitement," Daphne replied. "What do you have in mind, I have never been with a woman if that is what you're asking me?" Daphne continued, "and I have to say, you really aren't my type, sorry."

"Oh, you're so off the mark, Daphne! No not that, not even close, something much more exhilarating and certainly dangerous. If I said to you that I was looking for someone with international contacts, what would you say?"

"I would have to say yes, I have that."

"And you're bored, yes?"

"Yes, I am."

"Do you have anyone in mind that would be willing to buy certain items, like art, jewellery and other possible items?"

"As it happens, yes, I do. My husband actually deals with some very... unscrupulous people around the world."

"Really? Then you could well be the person I am looking for. I need to sell these, but not in any country in Europe." I handed her a few diamonds to see her reaction.

"Are they stolen? Is that what you do, steal?" she asked me.

"Well, yes, among other things. Items such as these are stolen from German officers and other places."

"How lovely. Yes, I can sell these, is this all you have?" Daphne asked.

"No, but before I give you them all and also leave them with you, I need to tell you something important. I don't work alone; the other people I work with are trained killers. If you decide to play any type of games with me then they will track you down and kill everyone you care about, then torture and kill you. Knowing this, are you still interested?"

"Really? Wow, this is something else, just what I need in my life! Yes, yes, yes, I am in!" Daphne excitedly announced and hugged me affectionately, whispering, "Thank you," several times in my ear.

"Here are the rest of them," passing over the rest. "How long before you can get rid of them?"

"We are going to America on Monday for a couple of days to visit one of our factories, so whilst Leon is busy with that, I will deal with this. How much do I get from this?"

"How much do you want?" I enquired.

"30%?"

"Oh no, no way, 10%."

"Let's agree on 15%, it's a nice figure."

We shook hands and Daphne hugged me some more. I could see from her eyes she was excited. I just hoped she could keep her cool – only time would tell!

After spending the remainder of the day drinking champagne, I ended up having to stay the night at Daphne's, waking the next morning with a hangover that I just couldn't seem to shift as I made my way home.

Hannah

"Petra, we are nearing the drop point, one last equipment check."

"I really don't like this, Hannah."

"We are doing this, that's it, Petra."

The pilot gave the countdown and we jumped together into the darkness. I looked up and made sure my canopy had opened, and then scanned the night sky for Petra. She was below me and it looked like we were on target for the clearing.

One thing going through my head whilst we descended slowly towards the ground was just how vulnerable I felt. The sky was clear; my white canopy must have stood out from the darkness. All it took was for a soldier to see it and start shouting. To be honest, my heart was pumping so fast right at that moment...

We were down and Petra and I gathered our chutes and headed for the tree line. As we approached a figure appeared out of the darkness. It was our resistance contact; he had prepared a hole for our chutes in the woods.

"I don't want to ever do that again, Hannah." I had heard Petra puke after landing.

"I have to agree Petra, night jumping is not nice. At least it's over now - let's get to the chateau."

An hour later, we rendezvoused with the rest of the resistance fighters and we went over our plan. They assured me they would be in place and on time, so Petra and I changed into our evening dress and one of the resistance fighters, acting as our chauffeur, took us to the chateau.

As we travelled up the narrow drive the chateau came into view. It was lit up quite brightly and I noticed something different.

"Petra, there's two guards at the front door, they weren't in the intelligence."

"No. If they ask, we are from the town and are here as entertainment for the officers."

"Yes, that should work, Petra. But just in case. Be ready."

Our driver pulled up at the bottom of the steps leading to the door, and as he did so one of the guards came down and opened the car door.

"Good evening, ladies," he said as he held his hand out to assist me out of the vehicle.

I stepped out and he did the same for Petra now with a smile on his face - he obviously liked what he was looking at.

We headed up the steps and suddenly the other guard moved in front of the door.

"Papers, please," he said, holding out his hand. "Why are you here?" he asked.

Gesturing with my hand over my body I replied, "Entertainment."

He handed our papers back with an agreeable smile.

As we entered the chateau, I did a quick scan of the ground floor. It was laid out exactly as shown on the plan. We headed for the bar and got a drink, we then walked around conversing with a few people as though we were supposed to be there. Not too long to wait until zero hour! Checking my watch, the resistance fighters should now all be in place. Just as I looked up to give Petra a slight nod to get ready the air raid sirens started going off and we were plunged into darkness.

"Petra, radio room!" The bloody RAF were early!

Total hysteria kicked in, women screaming and male voices from the darkness shouting "schnell, schnell, to the bunker!" with soldiers and staff lighting the way with torches. It actually didn't take too long for them all to get down the two staircases. Petra and I hung back, so we were the last ones down the stairs.

"It's working, Hannah," Petra whispered in my ear as we descended.

As I came off the last step, I faked a trip and as I expected, they didn't really care about anyone else but

221

themselves. They shut and locked the door to the shelter. I pulled my pistol and shot the guard.

"Okay, Petra, place the charges and let's get out of here. I will watch your back."

We could feel the ground shaking as the RAF dropped their bombs, some I think a little too close. Our ceiling charges were set, and we headed back upstairs and for the front of the chateau as I pressed the detonator. Stage two was complete, but I thought we may have overdone it with the explosives as the whole staircase collapsed—but it's certainly sealed the door.

We were surrounded by the sounds of machine gun fire as the resistance cleared up those that didn't go down to the shelter due to lower rank or it was their duty to stay above ground. Petra and I headed for the air vents, slowly and carefully as German soldiers could be hiding in the shadows.

We linked up with some of the resistance fighters and they followed us to the barracks behind the chateau, four vents as shown on the map now came into view.

"Petra. Take two guys and start getting the tops off these vents, then find something to block three of them up. You three guys, come with me."

We headed over to the other side of the compound to do the same to the vents there, leaving one vent clear for the gas. By the time we were ready to throw the gas in all the resistance fighters had completed their mission and were now ready to leave. They didn't hang around - hit and run was their preferred method.

"Okay, Petra, put your gas mask on, go back to the clear vent, puncture the canisters and throw them down the vent, quickly followed by bunging up the top to prevent it escaping."

"Don't worry Hannah, I have this."

Once Petra was back in place, I shouted 'one, two, three' and the gas was sent down the shaft, immediately followed by us covering the vent.

I could picture in my mind the current scene in the bunker as they realised what was now happening; the struggling to escape, holding their breath, trying not to breath in the gas. It should be total mayhem for the first few seconds until the gas started to get a hold of them. Then slowly but surely, one by one they would stop screaming and struggling as they took their last lethal breath.

Petra and I headed back towards the front of the chateau.

"Now that is payback! Hannah, I actually kind of enjoyed that."

"Yes, Petra, I have to agree. If you're going to kill Germans, then that must be one of the top ways to do it. Now let's have a quick look around for anything valuable before we get out of here. Remember, money and jewellery only because we need to move quickly."

"Okay, Hannah, meet back here in ten minutes."

However, I quickly came to realise that although working with the resistance was a must in some cases, they also required funds for food and other essentials and so they hadn't left anything behind for us. I guess the spoils went to them this time.

"Hannah, the bloody resistance has taken everything, nothing is left! They have even taken every scrap of food."

"Well, you just can't trust anyone in war time. Let's get out of here. At least they left us a car, we don't have to walk to the train station."

Petra looked at the vehicle with disdain. "Oh, how wonderful. We can't sell this piece of crap though."

"Just remember, we have the diamond sale coming in soon. That should keep us going for some time. We also have all the jewellery from the other Nazis that we have collected over the past few weeks. We have enough for now."

"I guess you're right, Hannah."

We arrived at the train station and had an hour or so to wait, which was a good thing as we were both still shaking with adrenaline. Sure, killing gets easier the more you do it, but you can't stop the chemical reaction within your body. As we waited for the train, I couldn't help but wonder how Heidi was getting on and my mind started to fill with images of luxury, of laying under the sunlit sky in a place where there was no war, no death and destruction. Then I remembered my scarred body and was instantly transported back to the reality of my life and the fact that no matter how much money I had, nothing could change the fact that I would spend the rest of my life alone, never to be touched by the hand of love again.

The train was late, we couldn't stay on the platform for too much longer as it would draw attention from the guards, so we decided to steal a car and drive through the night to another city closer to our destination. Milan, Italy was an excellent choice and we would arrive there by 10.00 in the morning.

The drive was boring and uneventful. Petra and I took it in turns to get some sleep. Luckily, we actually made good time and arrived on the outskirts of Milan at 08.40. We decided to ditch the car and use public transport to reach the station.

"It seems we have arrived during some kind of troop movement, Hannah."

"This isn't going to be easy. Good job we don't have anything on us Petra, stay calm and we will be alright."

"Alright?! There are thousands of troops, more guards checking everyone going through to the trains, and look there are the Gestapo, picking out anyone they don't like the look of."

"A couple of well-placed bombs would thin them out a little, hey?"

"Don't joke, Hannah."

"Come on, we will be fine, all our papers are in order."

I took Petra by the arm and we strolled up to the ticket booth and bought our tickets, then headed straight for our platform. I couldn't help but wonder where all these troops were going thoug—south, I hoped. I was right, our platform was quiet, but this presented another challenge. It made it easier for the Gestapo to single people out and two young, good-looking women travelling alone would almost certainly grab their attention. Sure enough, within seconds of us sitting down they headed straight for us.

"Papers, please," said one

"Where are you going?" his companion asked.

"To Austria, to visit a friend," I replied, as I showed our documents.

They handed our papers back without another word and turned to walk away, then suddenly one turned back and started to open his coat. I expected him to pull out his pistol, how wrong I was...

"Can I interest you ladies in some American stockings or cigarettes?" he asked.

"How much?" I replied, thinking it would be a clever idea to buy something as it would get rid of him.

"I am sure we can come to a mutual agreement; it doesn't have to be money," he replied.

This didn't startle us in any way. After all, we were used to men of this type. The only difference was the surroundings, but this was the Gestapo we were dealing with, and they played many different games in an effort to catch you out. We didn't want to draw further attention or questioning, but we had to play this game carefully.

"Whatever do you mean?" I asked.

"You know exactly what I am talking about. You do something for me, and in return, I will give you a gift," he said with a leer.

"We are not that type of women, sir. Now, we will gladly pay you in cash," I replied.

"I can merely take you if I want. You do know that, yes?" he stated with a little anger in his voice.

"Yes sir, we both are fully aware of your power. This is a very public place, I am sure that the officers and soldiers over there would have something to say about it, especially once we start screaming rape!" I replied in a somewhat shaky tone.

This was an extremely dangerous game I was now entangled in. If he decided to simply shoot us or rape us, there really wasn't anything anyone can or would do about it - all he would have to do is label us as spies. Suddenly his colleague came over and whispered something in his ear, but he never took his eyes off us, not once. I grabbed Petra by the hand, awaiting his response and fearing the worst was coming. Without saying anything he closed his coat and they both rushed off to a different platform. I for one couldn't wait for our train to arrive and get out of there.

"That was a close one, Hannah, why did you choose to be confrontational with him?"

"Petra, we are personally responsible for quite a few deaths now. How do we know if they are now looking for prostitutes who kill German soldiers? We have no idea if they are searching for us or not, so I thought it would be best to come across as normal, everyday women."

"Well, that was a very dangerous game you just played Hannah, and I have to be honest my heart was pumping quite fast and still is."

"Mine too, Petra, but it seems we are in the clear." I squeezed her hand.

"Let's move a little further down the platform, blend into the crowd."

We only had a few minutes more to wait for our train, and we both let out a little sigh of relief as we watched it pulling into the station. We boarded as quickly as we could. It seemed to take hours until the train started moving, but it was only a few minutes. In those high-adrenaline filled moments the mind can play tricks on you.

We now had a six-hour train journey back to Heidi's. I was looking forward to hearing what Heidi had to say about her visit to Mrs Keller, as well as from Falcon regarding our next mission.

Chapter Fifteen

We were both quite tired now and were looking forward to a few rest days. As we approached Heidi's house, I could see Falcon waiting for us on the front porch.

"Another successful mission ladies?" he stated as we walked up the steps.

"Yes, it was very satisfying," I replied.

"Let's have a full debrief over a cup of coffee, hey?" as he ushered us inside.

For the next few hours we sat, going through every part of the mission with Falcon intensely listening to every word.

"You ladies are by far one of my most efficient groups behind enemy lines, and you have certainly got the attention of those back in London," he said, impressed.

"So, when are we going to be given code names?"

"That is something I will bring up with London and will get back to you as soon as I can, Petra. For now, you will have to be content with the fact that you have more than proven yourselves as a fully operational unit."

"Have you got another mission for us then?"

"Not yet, Hannah, we are scanning through a lot of intelligence at the moment and there seems to be several interesting possibilities coming up."

"Then we will wait to hear from you in the near future. Now, I need to get a bath and some sleep."

"I will be in touch, ladies; you can be assured of that."

To be honest, I really just wanted to get rid of Falcon because I was more interested in what Heidi had to tell us.

"How did it go with Daphne then, Heidi?"

"Very well. The diamonds are in fact in transit as we speak. They are back Monday evening and so I should get a call Tuesday."

"This is sounding very promising," stated Petra.

"Let's not get ahead of ourselves," I cautioned. "Yes, we are certainly going to receive some money, but we have no idea how much. Remember that we also still have all the other jewellery to get rid of."

"You're right, Hannah, but we have to face the facts. None of us have ever had anything, and what we did have the Nazis have taken or destroyed. We are due some good luck!"

"Yes, I guess you're right, Heidi." A yawn broke. "I am off to bed."

"Good night, Hannah," replied Heidi.

Petra just gave me one of those little nods and a smile. I wasn't really sure what the others were currently thinking about. Maybe they thought the money would allow them to leave this horrific world we had found ourselves in. I for one wasn't about to give this up, not for all the money in the world. For me it was about more than money, the money was merely a by-product of our circumstances.

Tuesday morning came around quite quickly and Heidi was on the train to Switzerland once again. She wasn't staying overnight this time and so we didn't have to long to wait.

Heidi

Daphne must have been watching for me coming up the drive, as she was stood at the door with what can only be explained as total excitement beaming from every ounce of her. It was so powerful she could hardly contain herself. She was bouncing up and down, with a smile on her face that could light up the world.

"Come, come, you're not going to believe this," Daphne excitedly stated, grabbing me by the hand and leading me into the rear garden. She was still jumping around like a schoolgirl.

I tried to calm her down. "Sit, sit, calm yourself."

"You're going to be just as excited in a moment Heidi, honestly, you're not going to believe what I have for you," Daphne replied.

Daphne handed me a piece of paper. On it was a series of numbers.

"What is this?" I asked.

"It's an account number, a Swiss account number, and in that account is your money. It was the best way to get the money out of the country, it's such a large amount," stated Daphne.

"When you say large amount, how much are we talking about?" I asked.

"One point two million," stated Daphne in the calmest voice she could muster.

I went deathly quiet, taking the brandy decanter and filling a glass, gulping it down in an effort to calm myself. "Just so I heard you correctly, could you repeat that please?" I asked.

"Yes, 1.2 million, and that is US dollars Heidi, not German Reichsmark," confirmed Daphne.

"Holy fuck! Sorry about my language! What are we left with after you take out your percentage?"

"That *is* yours, I have already taken mine," replied Daphne.

I was in shock, my hand over my mouth. I was shaking all over, that's more money than I could even count.

"Are you sure?"

"Yes, you can check it at the bank if you like, it's all there, and the same people have said that if I have anything else of value, they are happy to deal with me again," Daphne remarked.

I took another drink of brandy, another exceptionally large one.

"We must celebrate, Daphne, but another day, as I must return to Austria today. I will contact you later in the week and arrange an overnight stay if that's alright with you?"

"Certainly Heidi, I look forward to it."

"I am sorry I can't stay longer, but I must catch my train back."

I gave Daphne a hug and took my leave. I have to be honest. I really don't remember my walk back to town, I was in complete disbelief. I managed to pull myself together enough to remember that I should check with the bank prior to getting on the train. it was all about trust really, I had to check.

With a shaky hand I filled out the correct bank slip and handed it over to the lady on the counter. Within a few minutes she returned with the slip, folded it in half and handed it back to me. I thanked her and walked out.

Well, the account was certainly real. I hesitated to open the piece of paper which now had the account balance clearly written on it. I took a table at the café close to the station and ordered another stiff drink, clutching the paper so tightly my hand was going numb. With my hands still shaking I opened the paper and stare at the amount the lady had written. 1,200.000 US, I did a quick calculation in my head—that was almost 3 million marks. My journey home was a complete haze. The only thing I remember is tightly holding this piece of paper in my hand.

I arrived home late that evening, and the others were sat in the kitchen having a little food.

"How did it go, Heidi?" asked Hannah.

"All I can say is - prepare to be completely overwhelmed." I handed Hannah the piece of paper. "That is the account number of a Swiss bank account with our money in."

"Oh, that's a clever idea, how much did we get for the diamonds then?" Petra asked.

"It's on the bank slip Petra, I have checked, it's all there."

Both of them just stared at each other for what seemed to be hours, but in reality, wasn't that long. Petra suddenly jumped up and started dancing around, grabbing my aunt and waltzing her around the kitchen.

"Daphne has proven herself to be a trusted asset," remarked Hannah.

"Yes, and she is more than willing to take the rest of our stash when we are ready."

"How much is that, Heidi, in marks?" Petra wanted to know.

"Almost 3 million," I replied, enjoying the mix of emotions on her face.

"We should take a few days to let this sink in, Falcon should be returning any day now and he certainly doesn't need to know about this, agreed?" stated Hannah.

"Hannah is right, you can all do so many good things with all that money but it's best not to rush into anything," remarked Auntie. She always had been a level-headed person.

Hannah

Over the next few days, we discussed all kinds of possibilities regarding our newfound fortune, and of course the fact that we would add to it once Heidi delivered all the jewellery we had stashed to Daphne.

Heidi, of course, wanted to continue developing her skills in the field of intelligence. However, Petra and I just wanted to live long enough to see the Nazis defeated and continue to cause as many issues for them as we could.

One thing we all agreed on is that we were the only family we had now. Petra and I had come to see Heidi's aunt as our own; her hatred of the Third Reich was as strong as ours, and in many cases, she was our voice of logic.

The next day, Falcon and Viper arrived.

"Have you come with our next mission?" I asked in an eager voice.

"No, not at the moment, London is looking at several options as we speak," Falcon replied.

"We are en route to another circle - you're not the only ones we have to oversee," Viper chipped in.

"So, it's a social visit?"

"No. I thought I would let you know in person about code names and to see if you had anything in the pipeline from your own intelligence," Falcon responded.

Everyone turned and looked at Heidi.

"I have a couple of ideas, but that's all they are at this time. I picked up some chatter about the Nazis building some kind of underground tunnels here in Austria, but that's all I have right now," Heidi contributed.

"Well, look into that then, Heidi, and keep us informed. Now, codenames. London has decided that because you never work alone it is best you have a single name, one that reflects who you are."

"Okay. And what is that?" I asked.

"I think it's best for you to come up with that yourselves. London wanted me to express their gratitude for what you have accomplished so far. All of you have proven yourselves."

It seemed like hours had gone by during what was in fact only a few moments of silence, then Petra blurted out.

"The Blue Assassins - I like it."

"Yes, that sounds nice Petra," replied Falcon, who continued, "but we don't like to use the word assassin in any codename, it draws attention to your purpose and reason to exist."

"What about the Blue Ring?" I asked, looking at the others.

"Hannah, I like that," replied Heidi.

"Yes, I am with you both," added Petra.

"Then it's settled, 'Blue Ring' it is," confirmed Falcon.

And from that moment on the Blue Ring Assassins were born. Our ongoing objectives? Kill as many Nazis as possible and steal whatever we could, our lives are now full of new *hopes and dreams...*

Our fight against Hitler and his regime continues as we provide London with some overwhelming intelligence...

Blue Ring
Assassins
1943—1944
STEPHEN COHEN

Blue Ring
Assassins
1944—1945
STEPHEN COHEN